Greek Paradise Escape

Travel from the comfort of your armchair with Jennifer Faye's brand-new trilogy!

Nestled on a private Greek island, the exclusive Ludus Resort is the perfect escape for the rich and famous. But to the staff who work there, it's home.

Manager Hermione's job has been a lifeline since losing her home and family, so when new owner Atlas plans to sell, sparks fly between them!

Beach artist Indigo is new to the resort and has already caught the eye of one of its VIP guests, the Prince of Rydiania...

Concierge Adara spends her days fulfilling guests' wishes. Might it be time her own romantic dreams came true?

Make your escape to beautiful Ludus in

Greek Heir to Claim Her Heart
It Started with a Royal Kiss
Second Chance with the Bridesmaid

All available now!

Dear Reader,

Taking chances can be scary. It's why people often keep doing the same thing over and over again. This is the case for both Adara and Krystof, and boy, do they have things to work through.

Adara Galanis is comfortable in her position as the concierge at the Ludus Resort. She's been doing it for years and the guests love her. But when Krystof Mikos enters her life, he offers her adventure and excitement but without the commitment of a serious relationship. Despite not being the casual type, she tells herself that she's up for it...until she's confronted with the consequences of her decision.

Krystof Mikos is best man at his friend's wedding on Ludus Island. He worries his friend is making a mistake because Krystof doesn't believe in forever. But this wedding is the perfect time for him to fix things with Adara.

Adara doesn't want anything to do with Krystof, but when their friends' wedding starts to turn into a disaster, it just might take both of them to piece it back together. In the process, will they find their own happily-ever-after?

Happy reading,

Jennifer

Second Chance with the Bridesmaid

Jennifer Faye

Recycling programs
for this product may
not exist in your area.

ISBN-13: 978-1-335-73690-1

Second Chance with the Bridesmaid

Copyright © 2022 by Jennifer F. Stroka

For questions and comments about the quality of this book,
please contact us at CustomerService@Harlequin.com.

Harlequin Enterprises ULC
22 Adelaide St. West, 41st Floor
Toronto, Ontario M5H 4E3, Canada
www.Harlequin.com

Printed in U.S.A.

Award-winning author **Jennifer Faye** pens fun contemporary romances. Internationally published with books translated into more than a dozen languages, she is a two-time winner of the *RT Book Reviews* Reviewers' Choice Award and winner of the CataRomance Reviewers' Choice Award. Now living her dream, she resides with her very patient husband and Writer Kitty. When she's not plotting out her next romance, you can find her with a mug of tea and a book. Learn more at jenniferfaye.com.

Books by Jennifer Faye

Harlequin Romance

Greek Paradise Escape

Greek Heir to Claim Her Heart
It Started with a Royal Kiss

Wedding Bells at Lake Como

Bound by a Ring and a Secret
Falling for Her Convenient Groom

The Bartolini Legacy

The CEO, the Puppy and Me
The Italian's Unexpected Heir

Her Christmas Pregnancy Surprise
Fairytale Christmas with the Millionaire

Visit the Author Profile page
at Harlequin.com for more titles.

PROLOGUE

July, Paris, France

PITTER-PATTER. PITTER-PATTER.

Adara Galinis's heartbeat accelerated as the elevator slowly rose in one of the poshest hotels in Paris. That wasn't what was making her nervous. As the concierge of an elite island resort that hosted celebrities and millionaires, she was used to the finest surroundings.

Her racing heart had to do with the fact that she had traveled from Greece to Paris on the spur of the moment. She wasn't normally spontaneous. She liked things neat and orderly. Her job provided all the spontaneity she needed in life.

But she had a long weekend off, and in order to spend time with Krystof, she needed to come to him. Ever since they'd met at Valentine's on Ludus Island, they'd been casually seeing each other.

Krystof was best friends with the island's owner, Atlas Othonos. Earlier that year, when Atlas had briefly considered selling the island, he'd contacted Krystof in hopes that he'd want to buy the place. The sale didn't work out, but Adara had caught Krystof's attention. He'd pursued her in a charming sort of way—requesting concierge service and explaining that he wanted to dance with the most beautiful woman at the resort that evening. She was all prepared to extend an invitation on his behalf to whichever woman he'd chosen when he'd announced that the woman he was interested in was her.

She'd hesitated at first. After all, she made it a rule not to fraternize with the guests, but his warm smile and his enchanting way with words had won her over. They'd danced the night away at the Valentine's ball. It had been a magical evening that didn't end until the sun came up the next morning.

Now whenever Krystof stayed at the Ludus Resort, they made sure to spend as much time together as possible. At the end of each visit, he always asked her to fly away with him to some far-flung country. And though the idea tempted her, she'd always turned him down. She just couldn't imagine picking up and leaving without any planning. How was her assistant supposed to know what needed to be done? What if one of her regular clients arrived and she wasn't there? Part of her success was knowing the regulars and anticipating their wants before they had to ask her. She kept extensive files on their regular guests, from their favorite foods and colors to the names of their children and pets.

However, this weekend Hermione, her boss and best friend, had insisted she use some of her accumulated vacation time. Adara had been so focused on her job recently that she'd let her social life slide, and as for hobbies, well, she didn't have any unless you counted shopping.

So when she heard Krystof would be visiting Paris, the shopping mecca of the world, she took it as a sign. She couldn't wait to see him again. Their visits were so infrequent that it was always a rush to be with him. At least that's what she told herself was the reason for her heart racing every time she laid eyes on him.

She ran her hand down over the short, snug black dress. Her effort was a waste, because there was nowhere for the dress to go. It clung to her body like a second skin. It was a far more daring dress than she was accustomed to wearing. She'd bought it specifically for Krystof. She hoped he'd like her surprise.

As the elevator rose, her gaze focused on

the increasing numbers. With each floor she passed, her heart beat faster. All too quickly, the elevator quietly came to a stop on the ninth floor. The door whooshed open.

Adara drew in a deep breath and then exhaled. With her fingers wrapped around the handle of her weekender bag, she stepped out. The door closed behind her.

This plush hotel felt so far away from the privately owned island of Ludus. Of course, it wasn't a fair comparison, as the Ludus Resort had been founded by a former king—King Georgios, an amazing man who'd abdicated the throne of Rydiania. She didn't know all the details of why he'd stepped away from the crown, but once he had, his family had promptly disowned him. He'd moved to Greece and bought Ludus Island, where he would live out his days. It was both a sad and an amazing tale.

As she looked around the spacious foyer, she realized her initial assessment had been misguided. Though the wine-colored carpet was plush, and the fixtures were brass on cream-colored walls, that was where it ended. There was no precious artwork on the walls or greenery throughout the hallway. Whereas the Ludus was always looking to make the resort stand out in both big and small ways, it appeared this hotel excelled at a minimalist approach. Interesting.

There was no one about in the foyer. The only sound as she walked was the soft rumble from the wheels of her case. She couldn't wait to see Krystof. She was so excited. She hoped he'd be just as thrilled to see her.

The gold plaque on the wall showed that his room was to the right. She turned that way. Her footsteps were muffled by the thick carpeting. What would he think about her spontaneity? This presumed he was even in his hotel room. What if he was out at a card game or some other such thing?

She would have to phone him, then, to tell him she was here, and the surprise would be ruined, but she was jumping too far ahead. She lifted her head and noticed a stylishly dressed woman at the end of the hallway. The woman knocked on a door. Was the young woman doing the same as her and being spontaneous? She hoped the woman had as good a weekend as she was about to have with Krystof.

Just then, the door in front of the woman swung open. The woman stood off to the side, giving Adara full view of the person inside the hotel room. She stopped walking. The breath caught in Adara's lungs. Krystof stood there.

Oh, my! Her heart lodged in her throat at the sight of him.

His dark hair was spiky and going every which way, as though he'd just stepped out of the shower. His broad shoulders led to his bare chest. She was too far away to see if there were beads of water on his tanned skin. As her gaze lowered, her mouth grew dry. No man had a right to look as good as him.

He wore nothing more than a white towel draped around his trim waist. She swallowed hard. The only thing wrong with this picture was that she was supposed to be the one standing at his doorway.

His gaze lingered on the other woman. A smile lit up his face. The woman practically threw herself at him. They hugged as though they knew each other very well.

Adara blinked, willing away the image. But when she focused again, he was still holding the woman. So this was what he did when they were apart. Her heart plummeted down to her new black heels.

She turned away before she was spotted. The only thing that could have made this moment worse was if Krystof were to spot her. Her utter humiliation would then be complete.

Her steps were rapid as she retreated to the elevator. She wanted to disappear as quickly as possible. And lucky for her, one of the two sets of elevator doors swung open immediately. An older couple stepped off.

"Could you hold that for me?" Adara asked.

The gentleman held the door for her until she stepped inside. She thanked him. As the door closed, she recalled the image of a smiling, practically naked Krystof drawing that woman into his arms. Tears stung the backs of her eyes. She blinked them away. She wasn't going to fall apart in the elevator. All the while fury churned within her. Why had she let herself believe they shared something special?

It was quite obvious she was just someone to warm his bed whenever one of his other girlfriends wasn't available. How could she have been so blind? Sure, they had said this arrangement was casual, but that was in the beginning—months ago, on Valentine's. She'd thought they were getting closer—starting something more serious. Obviously she was the only one to think this.

She had been so wrong—about him, about herself, about them. She was done with him. Because his idea of casual and hers were two different things. In the end, she wasn't cut out to do casual—not if it meant him seeing other women while he was still involved with her. But it didn't matter now, because they were over.

CHAPTER ONE

September, Ludus Island, Greece

SHE WAS LATE. Very late…

Adara checked the calendar on her phone again. Her gaze scanned back through the days, one by one. She searched for the X that usually marked the first day of her period.

Day by day her gaze scanned down over her digital tablet. This wasn't the first time she'd been through this exercise, but it didn't keep her from wishing that she'd missed the little mark. *Please be there.* And once again, it was nowhere to be found.

Maybe she'd accidentally deleted it. Yes, that sounded like a legitimate explanation. Right now, she'd agree to any logical explanation—any reason except for her being late. Maybe she should have a backup plan. She would think that over for the future, but it wouldn't help her right now.

How was any of this possible? She hadn't been in Krystof's bed in months. After the episode in Paris, he'd messaged her to arrange for them to spend more time together, and she'd replied, telling him point-blank that it was over. They were finished. And then she'd promptly blocked his number.

Since her fling with Krystof, there had been no one else. Like it or not, she wasn't ready to move on. And she was certain she'd had her monthly since she'd been with Krystof. So what was going on?

She didn't feel any different. Just a little tired, but she credited her busy work schedule for her lack of energy. Not only was the resort hopping, but she had been training a new assistant for the past six months—an assistant who was now almost as good as her.

One pregnancy test later, and it was negative. Just as she'd suspected.

Two and three negative pregnancy tests later, and she was certain something was wrong. Hopefully it was just too little sleep or too much stress—something simple and easily remedied. Yes, that must be it. Ever since she'd seen Krystof with another woman, she'd thrown herself into her work even more so than she normally did.

She had known from the first time she'd met

him that he wasn't traditional by any stretch. She was so drawn in by his outgoing personality and the way he could make her laugh that she'd talked herself into stepping outside her norm and taking a risk on him. Maybe deep inside she'd thought she could change him.

In the end, she'd been so wrong about herself. She was a one-man woman not suited to casual dating. She'd also been wrong about trying to change him. Krystof had no intention of changing his ways for anyone. Looking back, she realized that she'd let infatuation sway her decision as she'd agreed to his terms.

And now she was the one paying the price. She'd let herself get too caught up in what might have been. The reality of him with another woman in his arms flashed in her mind. It was immediately followed by the ache in her chest. She refused to acknowledge just how much he'd come to mean to her.

Her missing monthly was the wake-up call she needed. She was in her thirties now. If she wanted a husband and a couple of kids, she couldn't waste her time on guys who didn't share her life goals. And Krystof definitely didn't want the same things that she did. He couldn't even commit to having an apartment. He lived out of his jet and a suitcase as he globetrotted around the world. Who did such a thing?

Her head started to throb. She shoved aside the troubling thoughts. It was so much easier to be distracted by her work than to deal with the gaping crack in her heart and now her missing period. Could things get any worse?

But first she had to get settled into her room at the resort. She was going to be the maid-of-honor for her best friend, Hermione. The wedding was going to be here at the resort in ten days' time. Both Hermione, the resort's manager, and Atlas had offered her accommodations until the wedding to make it more convenient for her. She had the bachelorette party to host and the final details to oversee for the big wedding on top of her usual duties. She planned to make Hermione and Atlas's wedding the most amazing event the island had ever seen.

This was the first time since she'd been hired straight out of the university that she was a guest here. Adara wheeled her suitcase into her temporary room. She couldn't believe she was going to be staying at one of the world's most prestigious resorts! As the lights came on, she stood in place, taking it all in. She wasn't used to living in such extravagance.

She'd grown up in a modest home in a small

village north of Athens with her loving parents.
They'd raised her to be responsible and sen-
sible. They'd also encouraged her to take the
position at the Ludus, even if it meant moving away from home. That's why when they'd
suddenly died in a car accident while on a
long-awaited vacation in Ireland, it had turned
Adara's life upside down.

For the past two years, she'd struggled to come
to terms with a life without her parents in it.
Their deaths had left a gigantic void in her heart.
She'd clung to her familiar life at the Ludus. Her
good friends at the resort had filled her days with
their warmth and companionship. She didn't
know what she'd do without Hermione and Indigo, as well as the other employees at the resort.

As her gaze took in her room, she couldn't
help but notice it was so unlike her modest little apartment on the outskirts of Athens. This
living room contained two white couches that
faced each other with a long glass coffee table
in the center. Decorations consisting of a crystal X and a matching ball sat on either side of
an arrangement of fresh-cut blush peonies. The
room's outer wall consisted of floor-to-ceiling
windows with sheers that could be opened or
closed remotely. At the moment, they were
open, letting in the sunshine from the skylights
overlooking the indoor pool area.

Ding.

The sound of an incoming message reminded her that she wasn't truly a guest of the resort but rather an employee with a very important job—the concierge. Her job was to make sure the guests' wishes were met and when possible exceeded.

Adara withdrew her phone from her pocket. She glanced at the screen. There was a message from Hermione.

Can we meet to talk?

It wasn't like Hermione to request an unscheduled meeting first thing in the morning. Something was wrong. Was it something to do with the resort? Or the wedding?

Sure. When and where?

Hermione responded, telling her to meet up in the penthouse apartment as soon as possible.

Adara left her still-packed suitcase sitting in the middle of the room. She would deal with it later. She headed out the door and made her way to the private elevator. You had to either have a key card or press the button to have someone in the penthouse buzz you up. As soon as Adara pressed the button, the elevator door opened. It was though Hermione had been standing there awaiting her appearance. Whatever was going on must be serious.

At the top of the resort sat the owner's apartment. It was huge and had the most amazing panoramic views. It was originally built by King Georgios. Seeing as it had all been designed by royalty, it was no wonder the resort loosely resembled a palace.

As Adara stepped out into the small foyer with a white marble floor and artwork adorning the walls, she had to admit the entire floor was truly suited to housing a king.

Hermione was standing at the open doorway to the suite wearing a frown. "I'm so glad you're here. Come in."

Adara followed Hermione inside to the spacious living room that was now a bit chaotic with wedding stuff all over the place, from favors for the guests to bridal magazines and decorations. But it was the two suitcases in the middle of the room that caught and held her attention.

Adara's gaze moved to her friend. "Are you packing for your honeymoon already?"

"No. We're getting ready to visit Atlas's father."

"Oh." Adara wasn't sure what to say, because the last she knew, Atlas and his father had a very strained relationship—to the point where she didn't think they even spoke anymore.

"His father is in the hospital, and I've finally convinced Atlas that we need to go to him."

"Oh, no. I'm sorry. What can I do?"

Hermione's gaze moved about the room. "Can you stay on top of the wedding? I mean, everything is planned. I know this room looks like a mess, but most of it's under control. I promise."

Adara's gaze moved about the room. Every surface was covered with boxes of stuff. Some decorations were complete. Other decorations still needed put together, not to mention the favors. "No problem. And if you need to push back the wedding until things calm down, I can help you with that, too."

Hermione shook her head. "I mentioned it to Atlas, and he staunchly refused. You know that there's bad history between him and his father." When Adara nodded, Hermione continued. "So he said he wasn't going to let his father ruin his wedding. I'm hoping with all of the time that has passed since they last saw each other that there's a possibility of forgiveness. I know it's a lot to hope for, but I'm worried that if it's not attempted now, Atlas won't get another chance for reconciliation."

Okay. "What else do you need?"

"Just keep everything for the wedding on track. There shouldn't be much to do. But if any questions come up, can you take care of them?"

"Sure. No problem." They really had nailed down all the details already. What could possibly go wrong? "When will you be back?"

"I'm not sure." Hermione grabbed her purse from the couch. She glanced inside, as though making sure everything she wanted was in there, and then she zipped it. "They were light on details about his father's condition at the hospital. All we know is that it's serious."

Adara could see her friend was worked up. She went to her and placed a hand on her shoulder. "It's going to be okay. Everything will be all right."

Hermione nodded before glancing around, as though worried she was forgetting something. "I guess we have everything." She turned back to Adara. "I'm sorry to just up and leave you with everything. Indigo said she would be around sometime today. She just got back from Rydiania. She can help you if you need anything."

Hermione rolled the suitcases to the elevator. As she stood in front of the open doors, she reached into her pocket and pulled out a key card. "If I'm gone for a while, you might need this to get to the wedding stuff. Make yourself comfortable. Like I said, we don't know how long we'll be away. Atlas thinks it'll just be overnight, but I'm hoping he'll change his mind once we get there."

"It's okay. I'll take care of everything. Don't worry about this place." Adara took one of the suitcases and rolled it onto the elevator for her.

"What would I do without you? You're the best friend I could have ever asked for." Hermione moved to give her a hug.

Adara hugged her back. "You're the best, too."

And then they rode the elevator down to the main floor. All the while, Adara went over the wedding to-do list in her mind. It all seemed doable, even if Hermione didn't make it back right away. No worries. She had this wedding stuff under control.

CHAPTER TWO

HE'D RETURNED TO Ludus Island.

Krystof Mikos had been avoiding the island ever since things had abruptly ended with Adara. No woman had ever treated him in such a dismissive fashion. The memory of her brush-off and subsequent blocking of his number still burned him.

But now that he was the best man in Atlas and Hermione's wedding, he didn't have a choice but to return. Though the wedding was still a couple of weeks away, he'd arrived early to steal away the groom for a long and extravagant bachelor weekend. It was his hope that he'd be gone again before he ran into Adara.

He had nothing to say to her after the way she'd ghosted him. He didn't even understand what had prompted her to act in such an outrageous manner. He could understand it better if they'd argued, but that hadn't happened. The last time he'd seen her on the island, their weekend had ended with a lingering kiss. And their final phone conversation had ended with him pleading with her to fly away with him. The destination could be her decision. She'd promised to think about it. So where had it all gone so wrong?

He longed to know the answer, but there was no way he was going to beg her to come back to him—even if he missed spending time with her. He was better off alone—just as he'd been most of his life.

He shoved aside the troubling thoughts of Adara. Right now, he had a bachelor party to focus on. He couldn't believe the man he considered a brother was tying the knot. He'd always thought they'd both grow old as bachelors, seeing as both of them had had rough childhoods and neither wanted a repeat of family life. But ever since Atlas had laid eyes on Hermione, his tune had changed.

Krystof couldn't help thinking that his friend was making a mistake. Sure, spend time with Hermione, have a great time together, but to pledge forever to each other—why?

There was no such thing as forever. Relationships didn't last. All you had to do was to look at the statistics, which would prove his point.

In Krystof's case, he didn't even have to see the numbers. The story of his childhood in northern Greece was proof enough. He never knew his birth parents. His earliest memories consisted of being shuttled from one foster family to the next. His high IQ had gotten him into lots of trouble, and he'd quickly been labeled a problem child.

His life was littered with short-lived relationships. He'd learned not to let people get too close to him—but there were two exceptions, Atlas and Krystof's foster sister, who had refused to let him disappear from her life.

Atlas had surprised him when he'd proclaimed he was about to be married. When he'd asked Krystof to be his best man, what was Krystof to do—turn down his best friend and tell him he didn't believe in marriage? Even he wasn't that heartless. And so he'd agreed to stand up for Atlas—even if he firmly believed it was a mistake.

And now it was time for them to jet off for a long bachelor weekend in Ibiza, which was one of the Balearic Islands, an archipelago off Spain in the Mediterranean Sea. It was known for its nightlife. They were going to have the most amazing time. He didn't exactly have a plan, because he liked to live life on a whim. However they decided to entertain themselves, it would be memorable.

He'd invited Prince Istvan of Rydiania, who'd

said he'd meet them in Ibiza. Krystof had also contacted some of his and Atlas's old class-mates from school. It'd be good to catch up with people and find out what had happened with everyone.

Krystof had just flown into Athens on his private jet to pick up Atlas. His hired car whisked him south of the city and onto a ferry that would deliver him to Ludus Island. When the car pulled to a stop beneath the portico of the resort hotel, Krystof made his way inside the lavish lobby with a white marble floor and a large crystal chandelier in the center of the spacious room.

He practically ran straight into Atlas. "Wow. Didn't expect you to be this anxious to leave. I thought we'd head off in the morning, but now works, too." He glanced around. "Where's your suitcase?"

Atlas frowned. "There's been a change of plans."

"Oh." This was news to him. But, hey, he was flexible. "Did you want to go somewhere else? I can call the guys and let them know the new location."

Atlas shook his head. "It's not that. I can't go."

"What?" Surely he couldn't be serious. "Of course you have to go. If this has something to do with Hermione, you can assure her that the partying won't get too out of hand." He sent him a big grin. Of course the partying would get out of hand. It was Atlas's last chance to have a good time before he was married.

Atlas arched an incredulous brow, and then he shook his head. "Do you really think Hermione's going to believe you would ever behave?"

"Why shouldn't she?" He wasn't that wild. He'd gotten most of that out of his system when he was a kid. "I'm a great guy." He planted his hands on his trim waist and straightened his broad shoulders. "Just ask anyone." His thoughts immediately strayed to Adara. "Maybe not quite anyone. But most people who know me love me."

Atlas rolled his eyes. "You definitely don't have an ego problem at all."

"Hey, I might resemble that comment."

Atlas let out a short laugh. "You're making this hard on me, but I can't do the trip to Ibiza. Something happened with my father, and we're heading there now."

That was the last thing Krystof had expected to hear. "Dude, are you sure you want to see him?"

Atlas shrugged. "Hermione thinks it's for the best."

"She doesn't understand. How could she? She wasn't around for all of the bad stuff."

His friend shrugged. "I don't know. It all happened a lot of years ago." He raked his fingers through his hair. "I didn't want to come to the island when my mother willed me this place. I was so angry with her, but while I was here, I found out that what I believed about her wasn't correct."

"But this is different. This is your father. He didn't just walk away. He made every day of your life hell."

"I know. I know."

But still, he was going. Krystof was worried about his friend. Nobody needed to go through that pain again. But it didn't appear anything he said was going to change Atlas's mind about this trip. All he could do was be there for him.

"What can I do?" Krystof asked.

"Hermione suggested delaying the wedding, but I don't want to. My father took a lot of things from me while growing up. I won't let him take this away from me, too." He shifted his weight from one foot to the other. "Would you mind staying here and helping Adara with the wedding details? I know something happened between the two of you, so if it's too much, I understand."

He would be alone with Adara? He wasn't so sure that was a good idea. In fact, he was quite certain it was a very bad idea. Then an intriguing thought came to him. There would be hundreds of guests for Adara to deal with, but he just might be able to pull her away from all that so they could talk privately for a moment—just long enough to appease his curiosity about why she'd brushed him off.

He could accomplish two things by staying: helping out Atlas and perhaps fixing things with Adara. "I'll do it."

Atlas arched a brow. "Are you sure? Did I mention there would be wedding details involved?"

"I heard." He was certain Adara would handle all those. She liked to be in charge and do things her way.

"And what about the problem between you and Adara?"

"I'll talk to her, fix things with her."

Atlas looked taken aback. "Are you sure about that?"

Krystof nodded. "Don't worry about a thing. I've got this."

"Really?" Atlas's dark brows gathered. "Where's the Krystof I know? What have you done with him? The last I knew you didn't do anything complicated."

"Maybe I'm changing." Had those words really come out of his mouth? The surprise showed on Atlas's face, too. Not wanting to dissect what he'd just said, Krystof rushed on. "I know a thing or two about weddings. Honestly, I can handle this."

"Tell me the last one you attended."

Krystof paused to think. He really gave it serious thought. There were frequent invitations, but he routinely declined them with the excuse that he'd be out of the country, because he was always on the go.

"See. I told you. There's something not right about you agreeing to stay here and help. And I bet I know why—or should I say *who* has you agreeing."

"Atlas, there you are. Did you get the car?" Hermione approached them.

Krystof breathed a sigh of relief that Hermione had interrupted the beginning of Atlas's interrogation. With a smile on his face, he turned to the bride-to-be.

"I was just about to when I ran into Krystof." Atlas moved to Hermione's side and gave her a brief kiss. "I didn't have a chance to call him about the change of plans, so I was just filling him in."

"Hi, Krystof." Hermione hugged him before

quickly pulling back. "I'm so sorry that this messes up your bachelor party plans."

"No worries. I understand. I'll message all the guys and explain. I hope your trip goes well. And feel free to take my car. The driver is waiting right out front."

They thanked him and promised to be back as soon as possible. He walked them out so he could retrieve his luggage. He wasn't looking forward to seeing Adara again—at least that's what he told himself.

And yet there was part of him that badly wanted to know where things had gone wrong. Since they'd been apart, he hadn't met anyone else who could garner his attention quite the way she had done. She'd grounded him. She'd actually made staying in one place feel all right for him—at least for a time.

Sometimes she was quiet, and other times she was talkative. She liked to share some of the fascinating details of her work—like the time she'd had to make preparations for a wealthy and influential guest to arrive at the resort via parachute—talk about going out of your way to avoid a traffic delay! She was very gifted in her ability to make people's wishes come true.

He wondered if a guest had turned her head. Did she have another man in her life now? Was that why she'd dumped him without explanation? The thought of her with someone else had his lips settling into a firm line as his gut twisted into a knot.

CHAPTER THREE

EVERYTHING WOULD BE FINE.

Adara should be smiling. After all, she was the maid of honor. And the wedding was going to be the biggest, splashiest affair this island had ever seen. She would make sure of it.

If only she didn't have this cloud of worry hanging over her. She regretted doing an internet search to find a reason for her missing period. Instead of it making her feel better, it made her feel worse. She didn't like the possibilities: hormonal imbalances or serious health conditions. What exactly was wrong with her?

She reached for her phone. She'd put this off long enough. She had to call the doctor. But when she got ahold of them, she found out she'd have to wait to get in. The earliest they could squeeze her in was the following Monday. It seemed so far off, even though it was only five days away. Five very long days of worry.

At least she would see the doctor and get her

answer before she had to deal with the next stressful thing in her life—seeing Krystof again. Since he was Atlas's best friend, he was the best man for the wedding. She inwardly groaned.

She hadn't spoken to him for over two months. She was still angry with him for being nothing more than a playboy and upset with herself for reading too much into their relationship. She wouldn't make that mistake again. Krystof was a part of her past—a painful lesson learned.

Thankfully, he wouldn't be here until next week, just before the ceremony. Krystof never spent too much time in one place, and without Atlas being on the island, there would be no reason for him to be here. He would most likely swing in at the last minute and then leave immediately after the reception. She could deal with that brief encounter. At least that's what she kept telling herself.

Lunch had come and gone in a flurry of special requests from guests. With her work under control, it was time to meet up with her friend Indigo, who was still doing a few special requests for drawings and portraits for guests of the resort. But Indigo's life was now quite busy, as she split her time between Athens and jetting off to Rydiania with her handsome prince—soon to be her husband. It just went to prove that happily-ever-afters did exist…for some people.

Adara made her way to her guest room. It was going to be her headquarters for all things pertaining to the wedding. As soon as she reached the room, she picked up her digital tablet. Her fingers moved over the screen, and then her gaze scanned down over the list of things to do.

They had worked hard to put things in order ahead of time. The to-do list was in pretty good shape. A smile pulled at her lips. This wedding was going to go off without a hitch. Then the image of Krystof with that other woman in his arms flashed in her mind. Okay, maybe one small hitch. And then a worrisome thought came to her. Would he bring the other woman to the wedding?

Her stomach soured at the thought. But in the next breath, she realized that bringing a date to the wedding would be tantamount to being in a relationship in Krystof's mind. It was something he would go out of his way to avoid. With that thought in mind, she breathed easier.

Knock-knock.

That must be Indigo. Adara closed her tablet and moved to the door. She swung it open. "Indigo, you're just in time."

The breath hitched in the back of her throat. It was Krystof. She blinked, but he was still there. "What are you doing here?"

His dark eyes stared at her while his expression gave nothing away about what he was thinking. "Aren't you even going to invite me in?"

A refusal teetered on the tip of her tongue. A glance over his shoulder revealed a number of guests in the hallway. She didn't need to create a scene. She opened the door wide. "Come in, if you must."

"Such a warm welcome. I feel like you really missed me." Sarcasm dripped from his voice.

She pushed the door closed. "What are you doing here? The wedding isn't until the end of next week."

He walked farther into the room and glanced around. Then he turned to her. "I want to know what I did for you to refuse to speak to me." His gaze narrowed in on her. The heat of his anger had her resisting the urge to fan herself. "You even went so far as to block my number." His voice vibrated with agitation. "You ghosted me. And I did nothing to deserve it."

Her mouth gaped before she forced it closed. Did he really think she didn't know she was just one of a number of women who passed through his life? Did he think she would be okay with that?

She crossed her arms. This wasn't the time for this conversation, not with Indigo about to arrive at any moment. "We're not having this conversation."

"You can't ghost me now. I'm not going anywhere until you explain yourself."

"I don't know why you're making a big deal of this." If he wanted to pretend he hadn't been seeing other women, then she could pretend as well. "It was a casual thing, and now it's over."

"It's another man, isn't it?" He studied her as though he could read the answer on her face.

She refused to glance away. He wouldn't intimidate her into confessing that she'd gone to Paris to surprise him and instead she was the one to be unpleasantly surprised. "If there was another man, would that put an end to this conversation?"

"No."

"Too bad. Now I have work to do." She turned to open the door for him.

"Not so fast. Hermione and Atlas sent me."

The mention of her friends' names gave her pause. Her fingers slipped from the door handle as she turned around. "What do you mean, they sent you?"

"They asked me to stick around to help out with the wedding details while they are away."

She couldn't resist a little laugh. "You're going to help with the wedding? You?"

He shrugged. "Sure. Why not?"

His insistence on staying to help made her amusement fizzle out. "Well, Hermione already asked me to stay on top of things. So as you can see, your help is not needed here."

"I'm sure Hermione has everything planned out, down to the table setting for the reception, but with so many details to keep on top of, there are bound to be a few issues that crop up."

"And you feel that you're the best person to deal with those problems?" His unwavering gaze and confident look irritated her. "I don't think so. You don't know the first thing about the wedding plans."

His gaze lowered to her digital notebook on the table next to him. "I bet if I read your notes, I'd get up to speed pretty quickly."

She checked the time on her smart watch. "Well, that will have to wait." She opened the door and gestured for him to leave. "I have another appointment now."

As he walked past her, he said quietly, "You can't avoid me forever."

Maybe not. But it didn't mean she wouldn't try her best. She leveled her shoulders and closed the door firmly behind him. She pulled her phone from her pocket and started running her finger over the screen as she messaged Hermione.

Did you know Krystof is here?

A couple minutes passed with no response. Adara made her way to the other side of the suite. How was she supposed to deal with Krystof without the buffer of Atlas and Hermione?
Ding.
Adara glanced at her phone.

Sorry. I meant to tell you that he arrived early. I hope it's not too awkward.

Her friend had enough on her mind. She didn't need to worry about Adara's dismal love life. It wasn't like she couldn't deal with Krystof. If only there was some way to distract him—like a high-stakes poker game. And yet there were none planned at the resort in the immediate future.

We'll be fine. How are things there?

Adara grabbed her tablet and moved to the couch. She sat down and opened her tablet. She needed to go over the list of things to do again. She didn't want to miss anything, especially with Krystof looking over her shoulder.

Atlas's father had a stroke. No details yet.

Adara closed her tablet. This was far more serious than she'd been imagining.

I'm so sorry.

I'll let you know more after talking to the doctors.

Don't worry about things here. I've got everything under control.

You're the best. Thank you!

Adara set aside her phone. How hard could it be to keep the wedding on track? After all, everything had been ordered and planned. All she had to do was make sure everything was delivered and put together. It would all be fine.

She just wished she could say the same thing about dealing with Krystof.

It shouldn't bother him.

And yet it did.

Krystof sensed that Adara was keeping something from him. It wasn't like her to be secretive, so if she didn't have a new man in her life, what was going on? And why wouldn't she tell him?

Perhaps she felt her reasons for not seeing him anymore were none of his business. He was the one who had insisted on having no strings between them. Now that he'd seen her, he felt as though they still had some unfinished business. And yet Adara had insisted on putting up a wall between them—a wall he kept failing to get around.

He'd been true to her in the months they'd been seeing each other. He hadn't even been tempted to see anyone else, not even in the last two months. Adara made him feel special—like she really cared about what he had to say.

They'd been having such a good time in each other's company that they'd kept it going for months, which was highly unusual for him. He hated to see it end. If he could just figure out the problem, he could fix it and they could keep going with their arrangement. He just had to get her to open up to him. But how?

He rubbed the back of his neck where his muscles had tightened. He was starting to get a headache. However, he wasn't leaving this island until he got some straight answers from her.

Buzz-buzz.

He pulled his phone from his pocket and glanced at the caller ID. It was Atlas. Krystof pressed the phone to his ear. "Hey Atlas, how's it going?"

"We just saw my father. He's not doing great.

We stepped out while he was sleeping to get some coffee. While Hermione is placing the order, I thought I'd check in and see how things are going there. Have you straightened out things with Adara?"

Krystof stifled another groan. "About that... ah...we haven't really had much of a chance to talk."

"What are you waiting for? I don't want anything to ruin this wedding. Not my father. And not your messy love life."

"Hey, it's not like that. We aren't a couple. We were just having fun."

"Did Adara know that?"

The question hung heavy in the air. Krystof swallowed hard. "Of course she did. We talked about it in the beginning."

"You mean the whole way back at Valentine's?"

"Yes."

It wasn't like their arrangement had had an expiration date, did it? Was that what Adara thought? Had she grown bored of him? Impossible. She'd enjoyed their time together as much as he had. He was certain of it.

Things had remained the same between them up until he'd texted her a couple of months ago to arrange their next meeting and she'd messaged him back, ending things. He was the one who normally ended an affair. He didn't like being brushed off. He really didn't like it happening with Adara. There was just something special about her, from the way she took great pains to care for those around her to her gentle laugh that warmed a spot in his chest and the way she made him feel like he was the only man in the room.

"Krystof, you do realize that the Valentine's ball was many months ago, don't you? And you've been seeing her pretty regularly ever since then. Maybe she thought there was something growing between the two of you."

He refused to see it Atlas's way. It wasn't like he'd ever said anything to lead her on. He wouldn't do that—he wouldn't intentionally hurt her. "We were becoming better friends."

"Is that all?"

Was it all? As soon as the question crossed his mind, he shoved it away. "Of course that's all. I didn't deserve her ghosting me with no explanation."

"If you say so."

"I do."

"Then keep your distance from her as much as possible."

"What?" Surely his best friend hadn't just warned him away from a woman, had he?

"I'm not messing around, Krystof. You've

done something to upset her already. You can't mess up again."

The stubborn part of him countered with, "And what if I don't stay away?"

A tense silence ensued. "Don't make me regret asking you to stand up for me at the wedding. I don't ask you for much. Just don't mess up my wedding."

"I won't." The promise was out of his mouth before he had a chance to think about the implications. Because even now, he was tempted by the memories of pulling Adara into his arms and kissing her long and hard.

"Thank you. I knew I could count on you. I've got to go. Hermione is coming."

The line went dead.

Wow. Atlas had never warned him away from a woman before. It didn't sit well with Krystof, but since Atlas was under so much stress with having to face his father again after so many years and his upcoming wedding, Krystof would abide by his wishes. Once he got some answers from Adara, of course.

CHAPTER FOUR

IT HAD BEEN a crazy, busy day.

Adara finally stopped long enough to take a full breath. Who knew so many people could have so many special requests while on vacation? But her workday was finally over, and the guests had all been taken care of, from needing a rare brand of shampoo and conditioner to providing a sunset helicopter tour of the island. When it came to Ludus guests, no request was denied…well, within reason. She'd been propositioned today—and she'd immediately shot down the advance from an international star who was twice her age.

She had only been propositioned twice in the entire time she'd worked at the resort. It was the first proposition that had been more like an invitation—an alluring invitation that she had been more than willing to accept.

As the memory of that long-ago Valentine's night filtered through her mind, she remembered being swept off her feet. Krystof had been attentive and charming. He'd been everything she'd been looking for in a man—or at least she'd thought so at the time. So when he'd suggested they start something casual, she'd surprised herself when she'd agreed. It was so unlike her, but there was something different about Krystof.

She shoved aside the unwanted memories. She wasn't going to let her guard down with him again. Fool her once, shame on him. Fool her twice, shame on her.

Her hope was that Krystof would grow bored at the resort without Atlas around and he would leave until the wedding. It wasn't like she couldn't manage things until Hermione and Atlas returned. She did not need him to help her.

Adara had made sure to review the wedding checklist twice. Everything up to and including the two-week mark had been accomplished. They were in great shape. And that's exactly what she'd told Hermione when she'd called not once but twice that day to check in on the resort and the wedding. Hermione really was a bit of a control freak. That's probably why the wedding couple had had the penthouse remodeled so they could live there after the wedding and be close to their business.

Chime.

It was a reminder on Adara's phone letting her know it was time to try on the wedding dresses one last time. They'd been delivered yesterday, but Indigo hadn't been available until now. So they'd decided to wait and try them on together. Even though Hermione was away, they really couldn't delay it any longer.

Adara was anxious to see the dresses again. Hermione had had both Adara and Indigo pick out the style of dress they preferred. They were simple and classic. The bride had chosen an arctic blue for the wedding color.

She texted a reminder to Indigo to meet her in her guest room. With the workday over, they would have a chance to check out their dresses without being rushed. They'd already had their final fittings, but with Adara now being in charge of making sure there were no foul-ups with the wedding, she wanted to try them on one last time before they put the dresses in storage until the big day. Afterward, she was thinking, they could share a glass of wine and catch up on each other's lives—not that she had much to share.

When she reached her room, she found Indigo pacing outside her door. When Indigo lifted her head and spotted Adara, she sent her a big smile. It was the same smile she'd been wearing ever since Prince Istvan had declared his love for her and placed a ruby-and-diamond ring on her finger.

Adara never asked, but she got the distinct feeling the ring was somehow related to the Ruby Heart on display in the gallery. Hermione swore that gemstone had something to do with her and Atlas finding their way together. Adara didn't believe in legends, but just to be safe, she was keeping her distance from the gallery and the Ruby Heart. She wasn't interested in a love match, especially after the way things had ended with Krystof.

"I hope I didn't keep you waiting too long." Adara opened the door to her room.

"Not at all." Indigo followed her inside. "How's Atlas's father doing?"

Adara placed the files and digital tablet she'd brought with her on the table before turning to her friend. "He's not the best. They're going to stay at the hospital until he's stable."

"That's a shame. I wish there was something I could do."

"There is… We have to try on these dresses one last time, and then I'll put them in storage until the big day." She glanced over, catching Indigo admiring her engagement ring. "Have you two set a wedding date yet?"

Indigo shook her head. "When you marry a

prince, a lot of the decisions are taken out of your hands."

"Oh, really? I mean, I just thought with him stepping out of the line of succession that, well, you guys would be pretty much on your own."

Indigo shook her head again. "You would think, but because he did step down from inheriting the crown, the king and queen are even more invested in making a big deal out of our wedding. They want to portray a united front to the world."

"So it's going to be a royal wedding?"

Indigo nodded. Her expression was blank, as though she hadn't made up her mind about how she felt about having the royals involved in her wedding.

"That must be so exciting." And then a thought came to her. "Hey, does this mean you'll be a princess?"

Indigo's eyes widened as she nodded her head. "Can you believe it?"

Adara sent her friend a reassuring smile. "You're going to make the best princess ever."

Indigo let out a laugh. "I highly doubt it, since I have absolutely no idea what a princess is supposed to do. And even when I figure it out, I'm sure I'll do it all wrong."

"Not a chance. You have a big, wonderful heart. You're exactly what the palace needs."

"I'm not sure they'd agree with you, since their son stepped away from the crown for me. Though he would tell you there were other reasons for his decision, I still feel some sort of responsibility."

"But didn't you say before that he's at last getting along with his parents?"

Indigo nodded again. "Yes, they're getting along better than ever. At least, that's what he says. I just hope he never regrets his decision to give up the crown."

"He won't. How could he? After all, he's marrying you, and you both have such amazing lives. Him with his charities and you with your art."

Knock-knock.

"Looks like it's time to try on the dresses." Adara moved to the door and opened it. One of the staff rolled in the rack with the dresses. After thanking him, Adara moved to the rack with the white garment bags. She checked the tags. "This one is yours."

Indigo took it and moved to the couch, where she laid out the garment bag. She pulled down the zipper and then uttered a loud gasp.

"What's wrong?" Adara asked, alarmed.

"This dress. It's not mine."

"What?"

Indigo held up the fuchsia dress with its many sequins and ruffles. It definitely wasn't the slim-fitting blue gown they'd picked. And when Indigo held it in front of her, it was clear it was both too wide and too long.

Adara turned to the garment bag that was supposed to hold her gown. She pulled down the zipper to find another fuchsia dress. Her stomach knotted up. Where were their dresses?

"Where are our dresses?" Indigo unconsciously echoed her.

"I don't know," Adara said.

With dread, she moved to the last dress bag. It was supposed to be Hermione's wedding gown. After the final fitting, the seamstress promised to fix a couple of the loose pearls and steam out any wrinkles before delivering it.

Please let this be the right dress.

Adara lowered the zipper. All the while her heart was in her throat. This just had to be the right dress, because if worse came to worst, they could find new bridesmaids' dresses, but a wedding gown...it was special. You couldn't just run out and buy a new one—especially with the bride away dealing with a family emergency and the ceremony next week.

She paused for just a second in pulling down the zipper, not sure she wanted to see the dress. Indigo moved to stand next to her. Adara pushed the garment bag back to find an ivory bridal gown with ruffles. Lots and lots of ruffles.

Hermione's beloved snow-white gown didn't have a ruffle anywhere on it.

Both Adara and Indigo gasped in horror.

Oh, no! This is a mess.

She told herself not to panic. This could be easily resolved. She would just call the bridal boutique. She was certain whoever owned these gowns wanted them back as much as Adara and her friends wanted their dresses.

"We should tell Hermione."

"No." Adara shook her head. "We aren't going to bother her with this. She has other, more important things to deal with at the moment. I plan to find out where our dresses are. Just leave these ones with me, and I'll contact the boutique to sort this out."

Indigo sent her a worried look. "Can I do anything to help?"

"Not right now. But closer to the wedding, I'll need your help making the favors and some decorations."

"I can do that. Just let me know when you need me."

Indigo returned the dresses to the rack and then left. Adara checked the bags for the name of the boutique, but there was no logo. She retrieved a stack of paperwork for the wedding. Somewhere in there would be the phone number for the boutique. For some reason she thought it would be right on top, but it wasn't. And to her frustration, she couldn't recall the name. She'd only been there a couple of times and hadn't paid attention.

There was a knock at the door. With the stack of papers in hand, she moved to the door and opened it. There stood Krystof. She inwardly groaned. She didn't have time for him at the moment. If she hurried, she might be able to reach the shop before they closed for the day.

"Unless this is an emergency, it's going to have to wait. I've got something important to deal with right now." She resumed thumbing through the pages.

"What's the matter?" Krystof's deep, rich voice was unmistakable.

She wanted to ignore him until he grew bored and went away, but she knew him too well. Krystof thrived on a challenge. And her ignoring him would strike him as a challenge to try and distract her from whatever she was working on. And she couldn't let that happen.

With great reluctance, she paused and looked at him—really looked at him. That was her first mistake, as her gaze hungrily took in his tanned legs clad in a pair of navy shorts and a white polo shirt that hinted at his muscled chest. When she drew her gaze upward past his broad shoulders, she admired his strong jawline and squared chin. And then there were those kissable lips that could make her forget about everything else but getting lost in his arms.

But none of that mattered now. The fling they'd had was over. She'd thought she could do the casual thing with him, but she'd been wrong. She was a one-man woman, and she wanted a man who was only interested in her. The memory of him holding that other woman in his arms cooled her warmed blood.

When her gaze finally met his brown eyes, she found amusement glittering in them. Her back teeth ground together. He'd caught her checking him out. Why had she done that? She was over him. It didn't matter how great a lover he was, he wasn't her man. And he never would be.

"What do you want, Krystof? Can't you see I'm in the middle of something important?"

"It wouldn't happen to have something to do with the wedding, would it?"

She considered lying to him so he'd leave, but what good would that do her? It was easier just to honest with him and send him on his way. "Promise this just stays between us?"

His dark brows arched. "Of course. How bad is it?"

"Well, considering they delivered the wrong

dresses for the wedding, it's definitely not the best news."

"The wrong dresses! How did you miss this?"

"How did *I*?" Was he serious? "I didn't miss anything. This is the first chance we had to look at the dresses. Remember, some of us have to work for a living." She glared at him.

His brown eyes grew stormy, but when he spoke, his tone was level. "How wrong are they? Maybe it's still something you can work with."

"Are you kidding me?" Then she realized he was perfectly serious. "No. We can't just swap them for the originals. These dresses are the wrong color, the wrong style and the wrong sizes."

"That does seem to be a problem."

"You think? Now if you'll leave me be, I'm about to call the boutique." She returned her attention to the pages of wedding receipts and forms.

She could feel Krystof's gaze upon her, but she didn't give him the satisfaction of knowing that she was paying him any attention. Her priority was fixing this snafu with the wedding before Hermione found out.

In this particular moment, she didn't want to talk to him. She'd already wasted enough time on him. Now she just wanted to pretend he didn't exist, but he was making that difficult as he stood there with his arms crossed over his broad chest and a frown on his handsome face. And that irritated her, too. No one that annoying should be so good-looking.

CHAPTER FIVE

HE SHOULD WALK AWAY. This was not his problem.

And yet Krystof could see the worry written all over Adara's beautiful face. Her brown hair with its blond highlights was pulled back in a braid that swept past her shoulders. A fringe framed her perfectly made-up face.

It was the stubborn jut of her chin and the firm line of her glossy lips that let him know she wasn't giving up until the dress situation was properly resolved—with the original dresses located and returned to her as soon as possible.

He honestly didn't see the big deal. After all, these were just dresses, weren't they? Surely they could buy other dresses.

But he wasn't so out of the loop that he didn't know some women invested a lot of effort and dreams into weddings. They had a vision, and it upset them greatly when that vision didn't come to fruition. That appeared to be the case here.

Thankfully he didn't have any intention of getting married. He'd already had enough people let him down in life. He wasn't about to open himself up just to be hurt all over again. All those vows about loving each other until death—he wondered how many people really believed the words when they said them. Did they really believe in forever? He categorically did not.

He took in the lines that now bracketed Adara's blue eyes and kissable mouth as she stood there with the phone pressed to her ear. As the silence dragged on, twin lines formed between her brows. It didn't appear the bridal boutique was going to answer.

When she disconnected the call, his curiosity got the best of him. "When do they open again?"

"I don't know. They were supposed to be open now."

"Maybe they're busy with other customers. Try again."

He expected an argument, but instead she once more dialed the boutique. She held the phone to her ear as she began to pace. Eventually she disconnected the call and shook her head.

"I don't understand," she said. "Between the three of us, we've been to the shop numerous times, when you include picking out the dresses and the fittings. They were always open during business hours."

He reached for his phone. "What's the name of the shop?"

She told him, and he typed it into the search engine. It took him a couple of tries until he spelled it correctly. And then at last the shop's website popped up on the screen.

He checked their hours of operation. "It says they should be open today until six."

Adara checked the time. "It's only four."

"Maybe we should go for a ride."

"Good idea. I'll take the dresses with me. I don't want to have to make a second trip." She reached for her purse and grabbed the dresses.

When she started for the door, he fell into step behind her. He was certain this mix-up could be easily resolved. After all, who would want a dress that didn't fit them?

Adara stopped abruptly in the hallway. He nearly ran into her. When she spun around, he was so close she stumbled. Her hands landed on his chest. He reached out to her. His fingers grasped her waist, and he pulled her close to steady her.

Time seemed to stand still as she leaned into him. He stared deep into her eyes as she stared back at him. His pulse kicked up a notch or two. For weeks and weeks now, he'd envisioned this moment. When he closed his eyes each night, holding her close and claiming her lips with his own was what he envisioned. And now he wanted more than anything to hold on to this moment—to make it last as long as possible.

His gaze dipped to her lips. All he could think about was how much he wanted to kiss her. The months they'd been apart felt like years. He'd really missed her a lot more than he'd been willing to admit to himself. But he couldn't give in to his desires—not with so much still unsettled between them.

His gaze rose to meet hers once more. He'd missed her smile and her laughter. He missed all of it. Still, he wasn't going to beg her to come back to him if she wasn't interested. Not a chance. He didn't beg anyone for anything.

How could she so quickly dismiss their perfect friends-with-benefits arrangement? Maybe Adara simply needed a reminder? Yes, that sounded like a good idea. His gaze lowered to her lips. They were devoid of any lipstick or gloss, as though she'd been caught off guard that morning and forgotten to put it on. Which was strange, because Adara was the most organized, put-together person he knew. He wondered what had distracted her.

He had always loved to be her distraction, but she hadn't given him the time of day since he'd arrived. And as much as he wanted to kiss her, he refused to do that until things were settled between them.

It was with the greatest regret that he released his hold on her and took a step back. It was though that's all it took for Adara to regain her senses.

She frowned fiercely at him. "What are you doing?"

"Keeping you from falling."

"Not that. Why are you following me?"

"Um…" Was this a trick question? "I'm walking with you to the car."

She shook her head. "No, you're not."

"Of course I am. We have to get this dress thing sorted."

"*We* aren't doing anything. I'm going to go take care of this. You…well, you can go sit on the beach or find a card game to play." She turned and continued to walk away.

Cards didn't mean that much to him, at least not these days. Years ago, they'd been a quick way for him to climb his way out of poverty. With a photogenic memory and a high IQ, which had earned him a scholarship to a top university, he'd found he was good at card games. Very good.

These days playing cards just didn't hold a challenge like they used to. He'd never told anyone this. He simply let everyone assume he traveled from one card game to the next. In truth, he just liked to travel. Sometimes he played, but often he worked on his computer programing. Utilizing computer language was like a puzzle to him, and it challenged him in a way that cards never had.

He'd developed a social media platform called MyPost. At first it had been a way to connect card sharks and arrange large tournaments. Then MyPost had started to grow. Now he had a staff that managed the site for him, allowing him to continue his nomadic ways.

He continued to follow Adara. "I'm going with you."

This time when she stopped, he was ready for her and had left enough room between them. She turned to him with an exasperated sigh. "Are you really going to stick around until the wedding?"

"I am."

Adara dramatically rolled her eyes. "Is there anything I can say to dissuade you?"

"No." He made a point of checking his Rolex. "We're wasting time."

Her gaze narrowed as she was silent for a moment. "Fine. But when we get there, I'll do the talking."

"Be my guest." But he planned to do some talking before they arrived at the boutique.

She glared at him. "Has anyone ever told you that you're stubborn?"

"Yes."

With a deep sigh, she held out the dresses to him. "If you insist on coming with me, you can make yourself useful." When he took the dresses from her, she said, "Hold them higher. They can't touch the ground." When he went to drape them over his arm, she frowned. "They'll get wrinkled that way."

Was she serious? They weren't even her dresses. "Why do you care?"

"Because if I was the person that owned those dresses, I'd hope someone would take good care of them."

He lifted the dresses until she was satisfied. Then she turned and continued walking. She pulled out her phone and made a call. "Demi, an emergency has come up. I need to step out for a bit. Can you handle things here?" Her head bobbed up and down as though she were agreeing with whatever was said on the other end of the phone. "Thank you. I appreciate this."

"Everything okay?" he asked.

"With the resort, yes. As for the wedding, it will be fine as soon as we find the correct dresses."

When they came to the end of the hallway, instead of turning right to head to the lobby, Adara turned to the left. He was confused. "I thought we were leaving."

"We are. My car is parked in the back."

"But why don't we just take one of the resort's sedans?"

"Because those are for guests." She kept walking.

He hurried to keep up with her. "Of which I happen to be one."

"But I'm not."

"Really? Because I'd heard from Atlas that you're staying at the resort until the wedding."

"That's just a matter of convenience. I'm not a true guest." She stopped at the exit and turned to him. "Must we do this?"

"Do what?"

"Talk. It'd be so much easier if I was doing this alone." And then she slipped on her sunglasses and headed outside.

He may have been warned off pursuing Adara by his best friend, but if he could just get her to stop long enough to really listen to him, he was certain he could clear up their misunderstanding. And then they could go back to their friends-with-benefits status. No one would get hurt, because emotions wouldn't be involved.

And this car ride was the perfect opportunity

to have a conversation. He refused to let the opportunity slip by him. He was certain that by the time they returned to the resort, he'd know exactly where things had gone wrong between them.

Why was he here?

Not the wedding part. She understood about his best man duties. But why was he in her car? Why was he inserting himself in the preparations when she was fully capable of handling them alone?

Adara had no answers. It certainly wasn't because wedding planning excited him. And it wasn't likely he was still interested in her—not when he could have his pick of so many other women. So was what he said true? He was just looking out for his best friend?

He'd just told her he planned to stick around until the wedding and seemed insistent he should insert himself into the wedding plans. But why? She wanted nothing to do with him. What about that didn't he get?

She needed to tell him point-blank that she didn't want him around. Maybe then he'd move on to his next card game or next beautiful woman. The thought of him with another woman in his arms had her gripping the steering wheel tighter. She refused to let her thoughts go there.

When they reached the ferry to the mainland, he took a phone call. She thought at first it was one of his girlfriends, and once again an uneasy feeling churned in the pit of her stomach. However, when he mentioned assets and liabilities, she breathed easier. A business call. She couldn't deny her curiosity. Was this a new direction in his life? She was dying to ask him questions, but she refused to get drawn into his world again.

With him distracted, she moved to the upper deck and approached the railing. She hoped for a little breathing room. Krystof was starting to feel like her shadow. She couldn't ever remember him being so attentive. In fact, she was quite certain he'd never been this persistent. Was it guilt? Had he spotted her back at the Paris hotel after all?

She'd never know, because she wasn't going to discuss that episode with him. To live through it was enough humiliation for her. She didn't want to rehash the horrible scene.

Was it possible he regretted the other woman? Did he realize what a good thing he'd had with her? It would serve him right if he had regrets. She had her own for thinking he could change.

There had been the briefest moment when

she'd first run into him again, when the episode in Paris had vanished from her mind. For a split second, she'd forgotten everything except how good they were together.

When he had gazed into her eyes, her heart had pounded so loud that it'd echoed in her ears. Her body had thoroughly and completely betrayed her. Because there was absolutely no reason she should want him any longer.

She'd been wrong to get involved with him in the first place. He was nothing like her. He acted without thinking. He didn't believe in making plans. He didn't even comprehend the use of a day planner. He liked to live on a whim. She could understand being spontaneous for dinner, but not as a lifestyle choice.

She liked to have everything sorted and arranged on her digital calendar, with its handy reminders. Every minute of her workday was accounted for, and she took comfort in knowing what to expect from her day. She didn't have to worry about where she should be and what needed doing, because it was already organized.

"I wondered where you'd gone." Krystof's voice came from behind her.

She inwardly groaned. So much for her moment alone to gather her thoughts. She grudgingly turned. "What do you need?"

"You."

Her heart leapt into her throat. His bold answer stood between them like a declaration. What was he trying to say? That he wanted her back? *No. No. No.* That wasn't going to happen.

She turned back to stare out at the sea. She concentrated on the swells of the water, trying to calm herself. Then, hoping her voice didn't betray the way his words had unnerved her, she said, "I'm not in the mood to play word games. Just go."

"No. I'm not going to be dismissed like you've been doing for the last two months." There was a resolute tone to his deep voice. "We're going to talk. It's long overdue."

She turned to him, noticing his arms were crossed and his lips were pressed in a firm line. "You have nothing to say that I want to hear."

"Too bad. I'm going to say it anyway."

She noticed how he'd waited until they were stuck on the ferry between Ludus Island and the mainland. There was absolutely nowhere for her to go to avoid him. She should have known his offer to join her today came with an ulterior motive.

She narrowed her gaze on him and jutted out

her chin. "Once you have your say, will you give me some space?"

"I can't do that. I'm staying until the wedding whether you want me here or not. This isn't about us. It's about Hermione and Atlas."

"Agreed. But it doesn't mean you have to be everywhere I am."

"I'm just keeping my word to Atlas."

She restrained a sigh. She wondered how much longer he was going to use that excuse. There was another reason he was sticking around. "Is that the only reason?"

"Of course."

"Because if you think you and I are going start up again where we left off, it's never going to happen."

A muscle in his jaw twitched. "You make it sound like you were miserable with me. I happen to know different. I know how to turn you on. I know the spot to kiss on your neck that makes you moan—"

"Stop!"

Just then the whistle blew long and loud, letting everyone know they would soon be pulling into the dock. With her face hot, she rushed back to the car. She'd wanted to tell him that he was wrong about knowing such intimate details about her, but she wasn't going to lie. The truth was that he knew far too much about pleasing her—more than anyone had ever known.

She didn't care if he followed her or not. That wasn't quite true. But she told herself that it didn't matter what he did. She was finished speaking to him, because he was utterly impossible.

CHAPTER SIX

SHE'D REJECTED HIM. AGAIN.

At least that was the way it felt after their conversation on the ferry.

Krystof wasn't used to being cast off once, much less twice. In fact, it had never happened before. He was always the one who did the walking away. And now that it had happened, he wasn't quite sure what to do about it.

His pricked ego told him to cut his losses and leave the island. Because Adara was completely and utterly organized. She didn't need anyone, including, apparently, him. The thought didn't sit well with him, but he refused to evaluate why it bothered him.

As for the wedding, what could go wrong? Okay, other than the mix-up with the dresses. But they were almost to the dress shop, and then the dresses would be sorted. In no time, they'd head back to the island with the correct ones.

With the bachelor party canceled, his services weren't needed on the island until the wedding. Between now and then, he could visit Singapore or perhaps head to Paris to work on his tentative plan to buy a tech company. He'd been putting off exploring the option until after the wedding, but why put it off when he could do it now?

And so he decided that, after things were remedied at the dress shop, he would go back to the resort to collect his things and then he'd be on his way. Atlas would understand, since he'd warned him not to stir things up with Adara. Yes, that's exactly what he'd do.

Adara slowed the car before gracefully maneuvering into a parallel parking spot. Krystof glanced around at all the colorful shops with their showroom windows painted with the stores' logos and the colorful awnings. If he liked to shop, which he categorically did not, this would be the area he would frequent. It was welcoming, and he appeared not to be the only one who thought so, because the sidewalks were busy with pedestrians carrying lots of shopping bags.

His gaze took in one side of the street before moving to the other. He searched for their destination. It was easy to spot because of the pink-and-white-striped awning with a wooden sign that read Dora's Wedding Heaven. In the big picture windows were mannequins—naked mannequins.

Where are their clothes? Aren't they supposed by wearing wedding dresses?

He wasn't so sure about this shop. It was an odd display, to say the least. And then he noticed the lights were out. That was strange, too. He checked the time. It was only a few minutes after five. The shop was supposed to be open until six.

"It looks like they've closed early," he said. "And they really should consider clothing their mannequins."

"Leave it to you to notice that." She rolled her eyes before gathering her purse. "I'm going to try the door." She got out of the car.

He'd come this far. He might as well go the rest of the way. And so he followed her across the street.

Adara made it to the door and pulled on the handle. The door didn't budge. She tried again. "I don't understand. Why would they be closed?"

He noticed the sign above her head. It read Out of Business. Well, that certainly wasn't good news.

He nudged Adara and pointed. When she saw the sign, there was a loud gasp. She took a couple of steps back on the sidewalk as though she were stunned by this turn of events.

"That can't be right," she said. "I just talked to them the other day to make arrangements to have the dresses delivered."

He noticed the phone number on the door. He tried it, only to find it was disconnected.

"Why didn't you leave a message?" Adara asked.

"The phone has been disconnected."

"That can't be right." She dialed the number and then held the phone to her ear. A low growl let him know she'd gotten the same response. She ended the call and looked at him. "Now what are we going to do?"

He noticed how she'd said *we* this time, but when he went to point it out to her, the worry reflected in her eyes silenced him. "They can't just hold your dresses hostage."

Adara once more stepped up to the glass door. She pulled out her phone and selected the flash-light app. He stepped up beside her. She held the phone to the door, letting the light reflect through the window onto the empty dress racks. The dresses were all gone. The store was completely deserted.

"No. No. No." Her voice filled with frustration. "This can't be happening. They seemed like such nice people."

"You don't know what happened. They might very well be nice people. We'll get this sorted." He hoped. "Let's go."

He turned around to find they weren't the only ones peering in the windows of the shop and asking questions. He cleared his throat. "Does anyone know what happened to the owners?"

The six or so people who had stopped in front of the shop shook their heads. No one seemed to know what had happened. This didn't bode well for them finding the correct dresses.

Once back inside the car, he checked the time. "Do you want to grab something to eat?"

She shook her head. "I have no appetite. What I want is to find the dresses for the wedding. How could this have happened?" She turned her head until their gazes met. "How am I going to tell Hermione that her wedding dress is missing?"

"You're not." His words were quick and firm. "She has enough to worry about."

"But I can't keep this from her forever. When she gets back, she's going to learn the truth."

"Unless we can figure out what happened between now and then."

Turmoil shown in her eyes. "Do you think we can do it?"

"I don't know." He couldn't lie to her. He had absolutely no idea what had happened to the dresses. Were they delivered to the wrong people? Or had the owners taken off with them to offload somewhere else? "All I know is that we can try our best to find them."

She nodded as she started the car. "We'll do everything we can."

"Yes, we will." He fastened his seat belt.

In that moment, he realized his plans to escape the island and the woman who'd rejected him had just been upended. Because somewhere along the way, he'd promised to help her resolve this problem.

And though he'd like to think it would just take a phone call or two to locate the gowns, he had a feeling it wasn't going to be that simple. Just as working with Adara wasn't going to be simple. But he would deal with it all, one way or the other.

This was the worst.

Okay, maybe not quite the worst. But it wasn't good.

Adara tried the phone number for the shop again and again. And then she started a search for the name of the owner. It wasn't as easy to find as she might have thought. Because the owner's name wasn't Dora.

Go figure.

The owner was actually a man. And when

she tried to find a phone number for him, she ran into problems. It was a common name, so she had a long list of names and numbers. This was going to take some time, and it was getting late.

Knock-knock.

Krystof stuck his head inside her office. "I thought I'd find you here."

She sighed and leaned back in her chair. "I've been trying to get ahold of anyone involved with the shop."

"And did you find someone?"

"No. And the owner's name isn't Dora. It's Michalis."

"Interesting." He stepped farther into the office.

"I've called a dozen people by that name, and they all say they have nothing to do with the shop." She turned off her computer. She needed a break. "How did things go for you? Were you able to come up with a way to track down the dresses?"

"I'm not sure. I have an idea. I'll let you know if I'm successful."

His words gave her a glimmer of hope when she desperately needed something to cling to. "Don't keep me in suspense. Tell me what you're doing."

"I'd rather not. It might not come to anything."

"Please. I've struck out all evening. I need some hope."

"I'll make you a deal. Come have some dinner with me, and I'll tell you my plan to find the dresses."

She arched a brow. "How can you be sure I haven't already eaten?"

"Because I know you, and you were set on locating the dresses. You wouldn't have stopped to eat. And that's why I'm going to make sure you have something to eat tonight."

"I don't think that's part of your responsibilities. You only promised Atlas that you'd help with the wedding."

"Um, but you're a part of the wedding, so I have to make sure you take care of yourself." This was his chance to dig a little deeper into what had happened between them. "That is, unless you have a date with someone else?"

She shook her head. "No date."

"What about a boyfriend?" He couldn't help himself. He had to know if she'd moved on.

Her eyes widened momentarily. "No boyfriend, either."

"Good." So if it wasn't another man, that meant whatever the problem was between them was likely fixable.

"Good?" She eyed him suspiciously.

That would teach him for letting his thoughts translate into spoken words. "Yes, good, because now you have no excuse not to join me."

She hesitated as though making up her mind, and then she shrugged. "I guess I can't argue about that."

He hadn't expected her to give in so easily. Every now and then she totally surprised him. This was one of those times.

"Then let's go."

She stood and rounded the desk. On her way out the door, she turned off the lights. That was a good sign. He was worried she was going to work all night trying to find the dresses.

"Where are we having dinner?" she asked.

"I thought maybe we'd dine in my suite. I already ordered food. It should be there when we arrive."

She stopped walking. "Krystof, I don't think this is a good idea. I told you we're not going back to the way things used to be."

"I heard you. I just knew that a lot of the resort's restaurants would be booked, and I thought you would be tired and want a chance to kick off your heels and relax. I promise I have no plans beyond that."

She hesitated, as though trying to decide if she should believe him or not. "Okay. Just a quick dinner, and then I'm off. I have an early day tomorrow."

"Sounds like a plan."

As they resumed walking, she asked, "How did you know what to order me?"

"It wasn't hard. We spent quite a few meals together. I know that you prefer fish or vegetarian meals. So I ordered scampi and wild rice with a salad."

Her eyes said what her mouth didn't. She was surprised he knew her so well. "It sounds good. And suddenly I'm hungry."

He liked the idea of them sharing a friendly meal. He held the door of his suite for her. He had been given the gamer-themed suite. There was a super-size flat screen on one wall with all the various gaming consoles, as well as a dedicated internet connection for online role playing. There were a couple of gamer's chairs that were so comfortable he would buy one if he had a place he called home.

The room was painted with graphics from various games. And a 3-D roulette table was on the ceiling. There were vintage pinball tables and early video games. On the other side of the room was a pool table, a Ping-Pong table and a shuffleboard table. And there were more games that he hadn't even gotten to yet, including a dartboard and a basketball hoop.

The best part was that the room had excellent soundproofing, so you could crank up the stereo system and play games the entire night without bothering the other suites. Not that he was into that these days. He found the idea of staying up all night and sleeping all day not as appealing as it had been in his younger years.

He noticed Adara taking in the room, kind of like a kid in a toy store. "I take it you haven't been in this suite."

"This is a large resort. There are a lot of suites that I have yet to visit. And they redecorate them on a regular basis. Nothing about the resort gets stale or, worse, old. Guests like to be constantly surprised. This suite looks like it was created for an overgrown kid."

"Did you just call me a kid?"

She shrugged. "I didn't say that, but if the title fits…"

He'd wondered how long it would be until she started to complain about his transient lifestyle. He'd told her from the beginning that he wasn't going to change, not for her, not for anyone. He'd always been proud of his easy, breezy lifestyle, without any ties to any one place.

But seeing as how she didn't want to resume their friends-with-benefits arrangement, he didn't feel a need to defend his choices. He did as he pleased. He had no one to answer to except himself. And up until that point, it was the way he liked it. But since meeting Adara, he was finding his lifestyle perhaps a little too freeing and, dare he admit it, lonely.

"I'm sorry," she said. "I shouldn't have said that. After all, you're helping me locate the missing dresses. I'm just tired, and there's so much to worry about."

So much to worry about? He was confused. "I thought the only problem was with the dresses."

"Oh, yes. Right. Don't mind me. I guess the hunger is getting to me, too."

She tried to cover for her slip, but he didn't believe her. There was obviously more going on than she was willing to share with him. He wondered what it could be.

"Why don't we play a game while we wait for the food?" she suggested.

She didn't have to ask him twice. "What would you like to play?"

She turned in a circle, taking in the numerous games. "How about pinball? I haven't played that since I was a kid."

"Pinball it is."

And so they took turns playing. He had to give it to her—she was pretty good for not playing since she was a kid. The more they played, the more the worry lines on her face faded and the more she smiled.

Someone knocked at the door.

"That would be our dinner." He moved to the door and opened it. A server stood there with a white linen–covered cart.

"Good evening, sir. Where would you like your dinner set up?"

"I think it would be a nice evening to eat out on the patio."

The young man, in black trousers and a white dress shirt, nodded. "Certainly. Just give me a moment."

"Not a problem. We have a round of pinball to finish." He turned back to Adara.

She pushed the ball-launch button. The screen lit up with flashing lights as the machine *ding-ding-dinged*. Krystof enjoyed watching her play. She was very focused on the game. And when she scored an extra ball, she gave out a little cheer.

For the first time ever, Krystof didn't feel the need to win. He'd already won by being in Adara's presence and feeling her happiness. He just hoped his idea to locate the dresses would work out in order to sustain her good mood.

Dinner was waiting for them by the time Adara's last silver ball slipped down the chute.

She'd won the round, and her big smile made Krystof grin, too.

They moved out onto the private patio where a table had been set with a linen tablecloth, candles and a red rose in a bud vase. Beneath silver covers was their meal, still warm, and the aroma was divine. For the most part, dinner was quiet as they each made short work of their food.

As they leaned back to sip their coffee, Adara asked, "What is your idea to get back the dresses?"

This was his moment for a confession. It was something he didn't tell many people. "I have posted it to my social media on MyPost."

"MyPost? You're on there?" Surprise was written all over her face. "I just didn't see you as the type to share things on social media."

"I actually developed the platform."

She sat up straighter. "What?"

For the first time, he felt awkward for allowing everyone to think he was nothing more than a card-playing nomad. He cleared his throat. "I write code."

Her mouth gaped. It took her a moment to gather herself. "Why is tonight the first I'm hearing of this?"

He shrugged and shifted his gaze to the moonlight as it played over the darkened sea. "Because I don't talk much about it. I guess

I got used to keeping things to myself when I was growing up. Without ever knowing my parents, I learned the only person I could count on was myself."

"I'm sorry. That must have been so tough for you."

He shrugged. "I never really knew any other way to be."

"So you went to school for programming?" When he nodded, she said, "Wow. That's very impressive. And you own MyPost?"

"I do. I've hired a team to do the day-to-day maintenance. It's gotten a lot bigger than I ever imagined." The site had millions of users that spanned the globe, and it was growing every day.

"So you're no longer involved with it?"

That was the thing. He'd had thoughts about ways he could expand it to make it more vital to a larger group of people. "When I started it, it was just a means to bring together card players. A way to plan and organize card games around the world. But I couldn't leave it alone, so I'd work on it in my spare time. It just grew and grew. And now it's getting so large that I either need to sell it or take a more active role in its processes."

"And what will you do?"

"I'm not sure I'm willing to give up traveling and be locked into one place."

"Oh." The light in her eyes dimmed as she busied herself with reaching for her glass of water. "What does all of this have to do with the dresses?"

"I've put up a post about the dress shop closing and asked if anyone else also received the wrong dress."

She set aside her water glass. "Wait. Are you saying you have that many friends on MyPost that your post would have a chance of reaching the right people?"

He shook his head. "I don't have any friends on the platform. I belong to a private card group. That's it. But I'm the owner. I can make the platform do what I want. And so I constructed a notification that has gone out to each and every user. When they log on, they'll see it. They will have to read it and click through to get to their page."

Adara reached in her pocket and pulled out her phone. Her fingers rapidly moved over the screen, and then there was a gasp. "You really did it."

He smiled. "I did. Now we have to hope it'll be seen by the right people."

She continued staring at her phone as her fingers moved over the touch screen. "And you formed a private group for all of those affected by this issue. There are already people in the group. We aren't the only ones searching for the right dresses."

"Yes, but so far no one has dresses like you're searching for."

Adara's gaze lifted to meet his. "This is wonderful. Thank you."

He shrugged. "It's not a lot. It still hasn't recovered the dresses."

"But it might. This is more than I've been able to do." Then twin lines formed between her brows.

"What's the matter?"

She shook her head. "Nothing."

"It's definitely something, so out with it."

"I was just wondering if Hermione would see it. Maybe I need to call her now and tell her what happened." Her fingers began to move over the phone again.

He reached out and placed his hand over hers, pausing her actions. "Don't phone her. The chances of her being on social media right now would be slim, don't you think?"

Adara paused before nodding.

"And hopefully the dresses will be recovered before she realizes anything happened."

"I hope you're right." She made a point of checking the time on her phone. "It's getting late. I should be going."

He wanted to ask her to stay. He wanted to pull her into his arms once more and kiss her lips. Instead he said, "And I have a card game to get to on the mainland."

A brief frown skittered across her face as she got to her feet. When she faced him, her face was devoid of expression. "I don't want to keep you."

"I'll walk you out." He had to rush to catch up with her quick steps.

She was mad at him *again*. And once more, he didn't understand what he'd done. Was he supposed to work all night trying to recover the dresses? At this point, he didn't know what else he could do.

At the door, she paused and turned to him. "Thank you for the help today."

"You're welcome. I don't know that I did much, but I have a feeling everything will work out." And then he leaned forward. He resisted the urge to place a kiss on her lips and instead pressed his lips to her cheek.

When he pulled back, he noticed that pinkness had bloomed in her cheeks. And as much as he wanted to pull her into his arms and kiss her properly, he knew it wasn't a good idea. She wasn't ready for that.

At least not yet.

CHAPTER SEVEN

HE'D KISSED HER CHEEK, not her lips.

What did that mean?

Adara had wondered about the kiss the rest of the evening and late into the night. She'd gotten to know Krystof fairly well over the last seven months. He was a man who knew what he wanted and wasn't afraid to go after it.

There was nothing in that kiss that spoke of passion or longing. And she couldn't deny that it disappointed her. She knew she should be fine with it, because they both wanted different things in life.

He'd obviously found what he was looking for in that other woman. She tried to tell herself that it didn't matter—he didn't matter to her. So then why was her stomach knotted?

The following day, she was thankfully busy all morning—too busy to have breakfast with Krystof when he stopped by her office. In fact, she'd come to work early today. It was so easy to be early when she was staying at the resort. Before Atlas and Hermione owned the resort, it would have been impossible for her to stay in a suite. There had been rules about the employees not being able to utilize the resort's amenities, from the rooms to the spa. But the new owners had seen fit to relax those rules— within reason.

She had spent the lunch hour in her office making phone calls to track down the owner of the bridal shop. And so far she hadn't had any luck. It was like the owners had just up and disappeared overnight. How was that possible?

Someone rapped their knuckles on the door.

She glanced up to find Krystof standing in the doorway. He sent her a smile that made her stomach dip. She automatically returned his smile. As soon as she realized what she was doing, she pressed her lips into a firm line.

"Hi. What can I do for you?" she asked in her concierge voice.

"It's a matter of what I can do for you."

"For me?" She had absolutely no idea what he was talking about.

"You know how I told you I set up that message on MyPost?" When she nodded, he said, "I've had a response. Someone has the wrong wedding dress. They think it might be the one we're hunting for."

"Did they include a photo?"

He pulled it up on his phone and then held it out for her to see. "I hope it's the right one."

"Me, too." She took the phone from him and stared at the image. It was the correct shade of white. The quality of the photo wasn't good enough to make out the detail of the beadwork. But the neckline was all wrong. Instead of the sweetheart neckline that Hermione had loved, this one had a square neckline.

Her heart sank. "This isn't the right dress."

"Are you sure?"

She nodded. "I'm positive."

"Oh. Okay. We'll keep looking. It'll turn up."

"I hope so."

"We should take pictures of the dresses you have and I'll post them to the group. The more eyes we get on the post in MyPost, the more people will talk about it. The more attention the wedding dress mix-up gets, the better chance of finding the correct dresses."

"Good idea. I've had them moved to my room so they were out of the way." She glanced at her calendar. "We can go now. I have a half hour before I'm supposed to meet with the Carringtons about their cocktail party."

As they walked to her room, the awkwardness between them returned. She had no idea how to make small talk with him, nor did she want to. If she hadn't caught on to the fact that he was seeing other women, would he have even told her?

She told herself that it didn't matter now. It was all behind them. She needed to stay focused on the task at hand—the hunt for the wedding dress.

In the end, Krystof was all wrong for her. Maybe it was the fact that something was possibly going wrong with her body. It had her looking toward the future differently. She wanted a real relationship. Something with strings and words of endearment. Was it so wrong to want someone to say *I love you*? Someone who wanted to stick around through the good and the bad? Was that asking too much?

Krystof had made it clear during their time together that he wasn't that kind of man—the kind who settled down. And for a time she'd thought she was perfectly okay with that—that it would be enough. She'd been wrong.

"Adara, isn't that your room we just passed?" Krystof's voice drew her from her thoughts.

She glanced around and realized he was right. She'd been so deep in thought that she'd walked straight past her room. The heat of embarrassment climbed up her neck and settled in her cheeks, and she retraced her steps.

"I… I'm not used to staying here yet." She let herself into the room.

Compared to his suite, her room was very modest. On the opposite side of the room from her white couches and glass coffee table was a king-size bed with an assortment of pillows in shades of aqua and white.

Although with Krystof in the room with her, it suddenly didn't seem so big—and the bed loomed large. She felt his gaze following her. She tried to ignore him but soon found it was an impossibility.

"I have the dresses over here." She'd had them place the cart into the spacious walk-in closet. She rolled it out. "We can just photograph them hanging on the rack."

"Or you could model all the dresses," he teased.

"Not a chance."

"Why not? I thought you wanted to get married."

"I never said that." Not to him, anyway. She thought some day she might get married and have a family of her own—something like her parents once had. But she didn't want to think of any of that now. "I'll just unzip the garment bag and fluff out the wedding gown."

She did that, and he took a photo. And then they did the same with the bridesmaid dresses. But as she was putting the wedding dress carefully in the garment bag, some of the material got caught in the zipper. As she struggled to free the material without damaging the dress, she pulled too hard on the garment bag, and the rack began to fall on her.

Krystof launched into action and caught the rack before it could touch her. When she straightened, she turned too quickly and bumped into him. She got a brief whiff of his spicy cologne. The scent was enough to take her back in time to a place where it would be so natural for her to just lean forward and press her lips to his.

Her heart started to beat quickly. She tilted her chin upward until their gazes caught and held. She should pull away, and yet her feet wouldn't cooperate.

The breath solidified in her throat. She couldn't remember why she was resisting falling into his arms and picking up where they'd left off. She longed to feel the passionate touch of his kiss. Because in that moment, she missed him so very much.

"Adara, where did things go wrong with us?" he asked gruffly.

It all came rushing back to her. His suggestion that they should have a casual relationship. His repeated requests for her to take time off work to visit him in various parts of the world. Her eye-opening surprise, the one time she'd done that, only to find him with another woman.

She shook her head. "Don't go acting like it matters to you."

"I'd really like to know."

Her gaze narrowed as she tried to decide if he was messing with her. Sincerity reflected in his gaze. He really didn't know that she'd seen him in Paris.

She sighed. "Remember how you kept asking me to meet you for a weekend?" When he nodded, she continued. "Well, I finally did. I flew to Paris in July, and I saw you with another woman."

His brows lifted, and then he stared off into space as though he were trying to recall the specific occasion. She started to wonder how many women he had on the side. Was she just one of a multitude?

"I don't recall seeing you."

She noticed how he ignored the mention of another woman. "You're right. You didn't see me. I'd just stepped off the elevator on your floor of the hotel. When I turned the corner, I saw a woman at your door."

His eyes widened. "Adara, you got things wrong in Paris."

"So you're saying I imagined you answering the door smiling, wearing nothing more than a bath towel, and the woman rushing into your arms?"

"No. I'm saying you misunderstood the situation."

There was a part of her that wanted to believe him, and it annoyed her that she could still be drawn in by him. "I think I got the gist of it," she said dryly.

"No, you didn't, because the woman was my sister."

"Your sister?" Surely she hadn't heard him correctly.

He nodded his head. "Yes, my sister."

Thank goodness she had the dress rack to hold her up. It took a moment for this information to sink in.

Krystof had a sister? Since when? From everything he'd told her, he was an only child who'd been abandoned by his parents. Had he done one of those DNA tests and found his sister that way?

Or was this just some sort of story he had concocted to try and fix things between them? She studied him for a moment. Krystof might be unconventional in a lot of ways, but she didn't think he'd outright lie to her just to have his way. With that thought in mind, she decided to hear him out.

"Okay," she said. "I'm listening."

For a moment, he stood silent. Was he surprised that she'd agreed to hear him out? Or was he trying to find a starting point?

He cleared his throat. "When Celeste found out I was going to be in Paris, we made plans to meet up. I had no idea you were going to surprise me with a visit."

And this was exactly why she didn't like to live spontaneously. Sometimes those spur-of-the-moment decisions worked out, but a lot of the time, they didn't. In her case, it most definitely hadn't worked out.

But if that was his sister, did it mean he wasn't seeing anyone else? Her heart leaped with joy, but her mind tamped down the excitement. There was something not quite right with this story.

"I didn't think you had any siblings." She narrowed her gaze on him, hoping to determine the truth of the matter. "I thought you were an orphan who didn't know your parents. Has that changed?"

"Of course it hasn't changed." He raked his fingers through his hair. "Celeste isn't my biological sister. She was another orphan. We shared the same home for years. She was a couple of years younger than me, and I would watch out for her."

The thought of Krystof playing the protective big brother thawed her icy heart toward him. But she wasn't quite ready to forgive and forget. "So you're saying there's nothing between you two?"

His nose immediately scrunched up. "Between me and Celeste? Ooh… No. She's like my sister."

"But she's not your biological sister. And years have passed. Maybe feelings between you two have changed."

Distaste was written all over his face. "Adara, I have no romantic interest in Celeste. She is now and will forever be the closest thing I have to a sister. Don't try to make it out to be something it isn't."

He was right. She was pushing too hard in her earnest attempt to keep the wall up between them. She took a deep breath. "I'm sorry."

"So you see it was all a big misunderstanding." He smiled at her triumphantly, and her heart dipped like she was on a giant roller coaster. He stepped closer to her. "Now can we at last kiss and make up?"

"No." The answer was quick and short.

She knew if she didn't stop this madness right away, he would wear away her resolve and then what? They'd go back to the way things used to be where they only saw each other when he had time to stop by the island.

And their phone conversations were intermittent at best. No. She'd already recognized that she needed a more stable relationship.

He reached out to her, his hands caressing her upper arms. "Come on. You know we were good together." He gazed deep into her eyes and lowered his voice. "Adara, I've missed you."

Her heart skipped a beat. It would be so easy to lean into him and claim his lips with her own. There was a part of her that was dying to do exactly that—but there was another part of her that knew a few stolen moments would never be enough for her.

She pulled away from his touch. "Um... I need to get back to work."

"I understand. I'll have these pictures posted online."

"Sounds good. Thank you."

"No problem." And then he let himself out of the room.

Adara stood there watching him walk away. She told herself repeatedly that she couldn't just fall back into his arms—even though that was what every fiber of her body wanted to do.

Still, she couldn't play by his rules. She couldn't do a casual, no-strings-attached relationship. Seeing him with that other woman—even if it had been innocent that time—had taught her that lesson. So why did she feel so disappointed that he seemed to have accepted her refusal so easily?

CHAPTER EIGHT

AT LAST THINGS were getting back on track, Krystof thought with satisfaction as he strode away from Adara's room. She now knew the truth about Celeste.

That was a good thing, because he didn't know how much longer he could resist kissing her.

Krystof knew Adara still wasn't convinced resuming their arrangement was a good thing. He just needed to take a different approach, that was all. One that drew her out of her safe and predictable life—one that showed her she needed to go after what she wanted.

He had no idea how hard it was going to be to resist her, especially when she looked at him with desire burning in her eyes. But he knew to act in those moments would be a mistake, because she was still putting up a wall between them.

If he could just convince her that they were good together, they could go back to the way things used to be. Lots of fun and no strings. After all, she had her career to focus on, and he had…

His thoughts stumbled as he realized he'd handed most of the control over MyPost to his very capable staff. And his interest in playing cards was waning. But there was still the chance to buy that tech firm in Paris. The only thing holding him back from doing just that was the idea of having to set down roots somewhere. There was still a part of him that felt like he needed to be out searching—no, exploring—exploring for the next big adventure and not locked in somewhere. A memory of his childhood being locked in a small room with no windows came rushing back to him. He pushed it away. That was then and this was now.

Later that day, Krystof stood off to the side of Adara's office as she spoke with a mother and daughter who'd brought in a wedding dress for Adara to examine, and in exchange she'd let them see the wedding dress that had been mistakenly delivered for Hermione. It would appear that though the dresses were a fairly close match, neither had the right one. This mix-up was far larger than he'd imagined. And so the search continued.

As the mother and daughter headed off for

dinner, Adara turned to him with a worried gaze. "This isn't looking good."

"No worries. We're not giving up. The page I set up for the dresses is just starting to pick up the pace. And now I'll add the pictures of this other wedding dress we've just seen."

"I don't understand how all this happened in the first place. How could they have mixed up so many orders?"

He shrugged. "I have no idea. I don't know if it was intentional, to take the focus off the owners suddenly closing up shop without delivering all of the gowns, because those stories are starting to crop up online, or if someone unintentionally mixed up all of the tickets with the names. I have a feeling we'll never know the answer."

"I feel like I need to tell Hermione now. That way she'll still have time to get another dress."

"A wedding dress? I thought those took months to order."

Adara sighed. "They do. But maybe she could buy one off the rack or find one at a second-hand shop."

"Do you really think that's what she'd want?"

Adara shook her head. "No. She loved that dress. She knew as soon as she saw it that it was the right one for her. And she didn't bother to look at any others after it."

"Then I think we need to keep looking for it."

Adara's gaze searched his for reassurance. "Do you really think we'll find it?"

"I think we're headed in the right direction." He wanted to promise her that they'd find the dresses, but he honestly didn't know if it was possible, especially in the short amount of time they had left until the wedding. But there was nothing more they could do right now. "Let's go get something to eat."

Adara's gaze moved back to her tidy desk. "I still have a lot of work to do."

He glanced at his Rolex. "And it'll wait. It's time to eat. Come on."

"But…"

"Adara, just leave it."

She expelled a sigh. "Okay." She followed him to the door and switched off the lights. "Dinner at your place? Or mine?"

"Actually, I have something different in mind." He presented his arm to her.

Her gaze moved from his eyes to his arm and then back again. After a brief hesitation, she placed her hand in the crook of his arm. "Where are we going?"

"You'll see."

They quietly walked through the resort. Their footsteps were muffled by the lush carpeting. On the walls were fabulous pieces of art. It was like walking through a museum. It gave Krystof an idea. Perhaps he'd start collecting art—finding the next big artist. Speaking of which, he'd already met a rising artist, Indigo Castellanos. He would have to make sure and purchase one of her works. She could be the start of his collection.

He paused to look at a painting of the ocean. "This is very good."

"I didn't know you were into art."

"It's a new passion of mine."

"Have you checked out the gallery yet?"

He shook his head. "I haven't."

"We could see it after dinner."

"Sounds like a plan." He smiled as he led her outside.

Little by little she was letting down her guard with him. In fact, they were almost friends again. His plan was working. That's good, because he'd missed her smile and the way it was so easy to talk to her about anything and everything.

"Where are we going?"

They continued to the other side of the patio and down the steps. He knew with all she'd been doing for not only her job but also the wedding that she needed to slow down and relax. And he had the perfect idea.

"We're going to eat dinner."

"But where? The restaurants are all behind us back in the resort."

"This is a special dinner. Just trust me."

When they reached the beach, they slipped off their shoes and set them aside. Evening had settled in, and the sun was hovering on the horizon, sending a cascade of pinks and purples over the puffy clouds.

"You want to go for a stroll along the beach?" she asked.

"Not exactly. But now that you mentioned it, it's not a bad idea." He tucked the idea aside for later.

He'd asked the staff to place his surprise for Adara just out of sight from the resort for privacy. So as they moved past a dune, he heard Adara gasp. He watched as she pressed a hand to her chest and gaped.

Candles lined a path of red rose petals to a table with a white linen tablecloth. A few torches surrounded the table, granting some light now that the sun was sinking below the horizon. The staff had done an excellent job.

"Krystof, what have you done?"

"I hope you like it."

"I love it." Her gaze briefly flickered from the table to him. "But how did you do it? I'm the one that usually sets up these special moments."

A smile played at the corners of his lips. "I may have sworn your assistant to silence as we devised this evening."

"Remind me to give Demi a raise."

"I'm sure she'll appreciate it."

"If I'm not careful, she'll be replacing me."

"Trust me. You're irreplaceable." He'd come to that startling conclusion in the time they were apart. She was very special.

They walked along the rose petal–adorned path. Adara stopped next to the table and turned to him. She tilted her chin upward and stared into his eyes. "This is beautiful. But why did you do it?"

A gentle breeze blew and swiped a few strands of hair into her face. He reached out, tucking those silken strands behind her ear. And then he gazed into her eyes. "I want to show you how sorry I am about the way things ended between us."

"You didn't have to go to all of this trouble."

"I wanted to."

He longed to pull her close and press a kiss to her lips. By the way she was looking into his eyes, she wouldn't have complained. But he knew it was too soon. She might kiss him now, but later she would change her mind. He had to be patient, and eventually she'd see that they were better off with their friends-with-benefits arrangement.

He mustered his resolve and moved past her to pull out a chair for her. Once they were both seated, she said, "If I didn't know better, I'd think you were trying to seduce me."

He smiled. "Is it working?"

"Wouldn't you like to know," she teased.

It was a pleasant dinner. No, it was better than that. He was captivated by her words and spellbound by her beauty in the candlelight. He didn't want the evening to end.

With soft music playing in the background and the lull of the tide, they enjoyed a candlelit meal. She told him about some of the more interesting aspects of her job, and he shared snippets of what he'd been up to in the last few months. Then the conversation shifted to his interest in art. She seemed genuinely enthusiastic about him starting an art collection.

"So if you were to collect art," she asked, "where would you keep it?"

He went to speak but then hesitated. He realized he didn't have an answer for her question. "I guess that would pose a problem."

"Unless you were to buy a place." Her eyes lit up. "You know, somewhere to keep your treasures and perhaps to call home."

"I'll give it some thought." Settling down wasn't really in his plans.

"You're frowning. I see you don't like that idea." Disappointment reflected in her eyes.

He owed her an explanation. Maybe then she would stop pushing for him to be something he wasn't. "I know you want me to stay put and create a home, but that just isn't me."

"But why? Everyone I know has a home, except you."

He sighed as he lounged back in his chair. He didn't like to dig around in his memories. Most of them were not happy ones. And though he knew he had it better than others, it still wasn't the happy, loving family that people witnessed on television sitcoms. In fact, his past was quite the opposite.

"I keep moving around because I was stuck in an unhappy foster home where I never felt I belonged." He toyed with the hem of the discarded cloth napkin on the table. "It was a place that I couldn't escape—no matter how many times I ran away." He stopped himself there.

He'd said more than he ever intended. He refused to say more. The past needed to stay exactly where it was—in the past. He never spoke of it. It was none of anyone's business. When he glanced at Adara, she was studying him. She was probably wondering about all the bits of his life that he hadn't told her. Even she wouldn't guess how bad it truly had been.

But it was better this way. He didn't want anyone to view him with sympathy. He was strong and successful. Maybe he wasn't the traditional version of a success story, but he'd created his own version of it.

CHAPTER NINE

HER HEART ACHED for him.

Adara quietly ate her tiramisu as Krystof drank a cup of coffee and stared out at the sea. He seemed lost in his thoughts. She wondered if he was thinking of his past.

She felt bad that she'd pushed him about his nomadic life after he'd gone to such effort to show her a good time. And the dinner had been fantastic. It was an evening she'd created for clients but never had the opportunity to enjoy herself.

And now it was almost over, and she felt guilty that she'd ruined it for Krystof. She wanted to make it up to him and put the smile back on his face.

As she took a last bite of the most delicious tiramisu, she considered suggesting they take a moonlight stroll along the beach. However, as she observed him, she changed her mind. She didn't think that was such a good idea. He was already lost in his thoughts of the past. She needed to get him to think about something else—perhaps a possibility for the future. And then she had her plan.

She wiped her mouth, set aside her napkin and then got to her feet. She moved over next to him. "Come with me."

He shook his head. "I don't think so. I'm just going to sit here for a few more minutes."

That was the very last thing he needed to do. The past had already robbed him of so much. It didn't need to steal any more of his happiness.

She reached out and took his hand in hers. She gave a tug. "Come on. It'll be worth it."

He arched a brow. "You aren't going to give up, are you?"

She smiled and shook her head. "Not a chance."

"Okay. You win." He stood. "Where are we going?"

"You'll see."

And so they set off for the spot where they'd left their shoes. Once the sand had been brushed off and the shoes put on, hand in hand they headed inside the resort. Along the way they passed numerous guests dressed in their finest clothes for dining at one of the three Michelin-starred restaurants at the resort.

She kept her fingers laced with his. She told herself she only did it because she didn't want him to slip away. But there was a part of her that enjoyed the feel of her skin against his. There was one thing they'd always had: chemistry. Lots and lots of sizzling, fiery chemistry.

The problem was sex was all they'd had. Sure, they'd had good times together outside the bedroom, but there was never any depth to any of it. Tonight had been totally different. Krystof had let down his guard long enough for her to get a glimpse of the man inside—the man with scars and insecurities. She had a feeling there was a lot more to his story, but what he'd told her was a start.

His admission dug at her heart. It was hard to hold him at a distance when he had showed her his vulnerabilities. She'd witnessed just how alone he was in this world—partly from a tragic childhood and partly from him keeping people out so he wouldn't be hurt again.

She wanted to help him—show him that taking a chance on a relationship was worth the risk. But she didn't know if she was the right person to coax him from his safety zone. After all, she was dealing with her own medical issues at the moment. But maybe she could help him with this small step forward.

She approached the large frosted glass doors of the Ludus Gallery. "We're here."

Krystof glanced up. "It's the gallery." He

stared at the sign with the hours of operation. "It's already closed."

Adara held up a key card. "I can get us in."

He shook his head. "I don't think it's a good idea."

"Sure it is." She didn't wait for him to argue. She flashed the card in front of a card reader, and then she had to press her palm to a biometric security device. The light on the reader changed from red to green. There was a click of the lock releasing at the same time the lights automatically turned on. "See. Easy."

She reached for the oversize brass handle and then easily pulled open the glass door. She held the door for him. Once he was inside, she closed the door and locked it.

He slowly walked around, taking in the various exhibits. He moved closer to the wall and lifted his chin to admire the gallery's latest acquisition. "These are really nice."

"I'll be sure to let Indigo know you said so."

"Indigo did these?"

"Yes. She has stopped working at the resort in order to pursue her art full-time."

His gaze moved along the wall, taking in the portraits of people in everyday life, from an older woman watering flowers to people at the beach and then one of children playing ball and lastly a baby. It was though each portrait displayed a different stage in life.

"These are quite impressive, but I'm sure she won't have time to work on her art once she marries the prince."

"She says she's not giving up her art, and Istvan doesn't want her to. He says he wants her to do whatever will make her happy." Adara hoped that someday she'd be so lucky. She wanted to meet a man who respected her love of her work that much.

They moved on to some pottery displays before viewing various pieces of antique jewelry. The gallery was expanding to the point where they'd soon need to build an addition. Krystof stopped to take in a series of seascapes. Each was the same scene but displayed at various times of the day. She stood next to him, taking it all in. She never tired of visiting the gallery. There was always a new display.

But tonight it was the man next to her that held her attention. She longed to show him that he didn't always have to be on the go, that he could stop in one place and not be hurt.

"How often do you get new exhibits?" Krystof's voice drew her from her thoughts.

"They've really been stepping up their exchange program. In fact, only about half of the gallery's pieces are here right now. The rest have been loaned out." She pointed to the left. "Do you see that large portrait with the tie-dye design?" When he nodded, she said, "That was borrowed from a gallery in Rome." Then she turned and pointed to another portrait. "See the portrait of the lion? It's made from thousands and thousands of seeds. I forget where it originated, but it's the most recent piece on loan to us."

"It's quite a collection." He moved nearer to the lion to have a closer look. "I can't believe I haven't been in here sooner." He turned and pointed to another set of closed doors. "What's back there?"

"It's where they have special displays."

"That sounds intriguing. Can we have a look?"

Under other circumstances, she would have made an excuse not to go back there. But since Krystof had emerged from his dark thoughts of the past, she was eager to do whatever it took to keep his thoughts in the present. And so she moved toward the back room.

She swiped her key card to open the door. While the front of the gallery was a large area with tall, white walls, the back room was much smaller, with black walls and spotlights that focused on the gallery's headliner.

This time Krystof pulled the door open for her. "After you."

"Thanks." She had to step close to him—so very close.

It would have been incredibly tempting to stop and turn to him. Kissing him definitely would have distracted him—and her. His kisses were so mesmerizing that they would often cause her to forget her common sense and lose herself in the moment.

But those moments were behind them now.

And with great regret, she continued past him and into the back room. She swallowed, hoping when she spoke that her voice didn't betray the fact that his nearness had gotten to her. "And these displays back here are royal jewels."

"Let me guess—they are on loan from Istvan's family."

"Actually, they belong to Istvan himself. He inherited them from his grandmother. And the Ruby Heart is the highlight."

Krystof approached the glass case. "The ruby is really large. Too big for a piece of jewelry."

She stepped up beside him. She couldn't resist getting another glimpse of the precious jewel. It was the most amazing gem she'd ever seen. With its many precise cuts, it was a work of art. The spotlights danced upon the various cuts, making it seem as though the gem had a power all of its own.

"There's a brass plaque with it. I can't quite make out what it says." He moved closer to try to read it.

She had hoped he'd miss that part. "It's really no big deal. There are more pieces to see out front."

As though he hadn't heard a word she'd said, he started to read aloud. "'The legend of the Ruby Heart. If destined lovers gaze upon the Ruby Heart at the same time, their lives will be forever entwined.'"

When Krystof's gaze moved to meet hers, heat rushed from her chest up her neck and filled her cheeks.

"Do you think the legend is talking about us?" His voice was low and deep.

"Krystof…" She meant to set him straight, but when his gaze met hers, the words clogged in the back of her throat.

He turned to her and pulled her close. It was as though she were having an out-of-body experience as she leaned into him. She tilted her chin upward. The breath hitched in her lungs.

And then he lowered his head, capturing her lips with his own. Oh, how she'd missed him. Her hands moved up over his shoulders and wrapped around the back of his neck.

It didn't matter how many times they kissed—it always felt like the first time. As the kiss deepened, a moan swelled in the back of her throat.

She didn't want this moment to end. She met him move for move. She opened her mouth to him. His tongue touched hers, and a moan escaped. He was amazing.

It would be so easy to fall for him. But she refused to let herself do something that foolish, because he'd made it clear he didn't feel the same way about her. What had he called them? Oh, yes, friends with benefits. He thought it was cute. She didn't. She wanted more—a real relationship with strings, complications and the hope for a future together.

His fingertips worked her blouse loose and touched the bare skin of her back, sending goose bumps cascading down her body. Her thoughts scattered as her heart beat so loud that it echoed in her ears.

And that's why she didn't realize they were no longer alone.

"Oh, Ms. Galinis, it's you."

She jumped out of Krystof's arms. Heat once again filled her cheeks. She drew in a deep breath, hoping it would calm her racing heart. Her hands moved to her hair, smoothing it. Then her fingertips traced her still-tingling lips.

She straightened her shoulders and lifted her chin ever so slightly as she turned.

She forced a smile onto her face. "Good evening, Christos. Yes, it's just me. I was showing Mr. Mikos around the gallery."

The night guard's forehead wrinkled. "You do know it's closed?"

"Um, yes. And we were just leaving." She quickly glanced at Krystof, who was wearing an amused smile at her awkwardness. "Weren't we, Krystof?"

"Yes. That's exactly what we were doing." He let out a laugh as he made his way past her and headed for the door.

The heat in her face amplified. She resisted the urge to fan herself. She turned to the guard. "Shall I lock up, or would you rather take care of it?"

"I'll handle it." He sent her another confused look, as though he still didn't understand why she would be in the gallery after hours. It was a first for her.

She didn't stick around. She walked quickly to the door. She was so anxious to be out of there. In her rush, she practically ran into Krystof in the hallway. "Oops. Sorry."

"I'm not," he teased. "If you'd like to walk into my arms again, I'm all for it."

She shook her head. "It shouldn't have happened. It was a mistake."

"If that was a mistake, I don't mind being wrong."

She lifted her gaze and frowned at him as he looked at her with amusement dancing in his eyes.

"I can't do casual," she said bluntly.

"I happen to think you do a mighty fine job of it." A smile lifted the corners of his mouth. "Commitments don't last. Forever is just a romantic notion. All we have is the here and now."

The image of him with Celeste in his arms came back to her. The searing jealousy that she'd felt when she'd thought he was interested in someone else meant she was in serious danger of falling for him.

She couldn't let that happen. She refused to set herself up for heartache when Krystof walked away. And he would. She was under no illusions about him ever settling down. Maybe not this week or next week, but soon he'd grow bored with her, and then he'd be gone.

She suddenly regretted bringing Krystof to the gallery. Not only had they been caught making out by the security guard, but they'd gazed upon the Ruby Heart together. And though she didn't believe in legends, she couldn't deny that

Hermione and Atlas, as well as Indigo and Istvan, had gazed upon that ruby, and both couples were now getting married. She suddenly felt nauseous.

"I… I'm going to call it a night." Her gaze didn't quite reach his. "Thank you for dinner. It was lovely."

And then, without waiting for him to say anything, she turned and walked away. She resisted the urge to glance over her shoulder. If she wanted to survive this wedding with her heart still intact, she had to keep him at arm's length.

The kiss only made him miss her more.

Krystof spent that evening in a high-stakes poker game that ran most of the night. He'd played on the edge with over-the-top bets and lots of bluffs, hoping the high stakes would distract him from his thoughts of Adara. It didn't work.

After sleeping late the next day, he was tempted to seek out Adara. He resisted going to her as long as he could, but eventually he gave in to his desire. There was only one problem—he couldn't find her. Was she avoiding him?

It wasn't like he'd set out to kiss her. It was a spur-of-the-moment thing, and she had been just as involved in that kiss as he'd been. His thoughts strayed to the Ruby Heart's legend, and he wondered if it had something to do with it. He quickly dismissed the idea. He didn't believe in legends. And it wasn't like this thing between him and Adara hadn't been going on for months now.

By that afternoon, he was ready to face whatever Adara threw at him. But before he could go in search of her, he had an alert on his phone that someone thought they had the bridesmaid dresses. Now he had the perfect excuse to see her.

Demi informed him that Adara was working in her suite. When he showed Adara the photo of the dresses, she said they looked like the right ones, but she wouldn't know for sure until she saw them in person.

The only problem was they had to drive into Athens to meet the person at their home. The ride was quiet, as neither of them broached the subject of the kiss. He didn't want to do anything to push her farther away. He was starting to wonder if his plan to put things back to the way they'd been before Paris was going to work out. Even though the chemistry between them was still there, as fierce as ever, Adara was fighting it at every turn.

In a surprise turn of events, the person did have the right bridesmaids' dresses, but not the right wedding gown. Now they only had one more dress to locate—and, of course, the dresses in their possession to return to the appropriate owner.

"Don't worry," he said as he navigated her car toward the ferry. "We'll find the wedding dress."

"I hope you're right." Adara's fingers moved rapidly over her phone as she answered messages.

With a mix-up at the resort to sort out, Krystof had offered to drive so that she would be free to deal with the problem. She was reluctant to hand over her car keys, but with a sigh, she did it.

Buzz-buzz.

"That better not be more bad news," Krystof grouched as he navigated her car through traffic.

She frowned at him. "Did you have to say that?"

He chanced a quick glance at her. "Why?"

"You've probably just jinxed us."

"Jinxed us how?"

"Oh, never mind." She focused back on her phone. "It's the booking agent for the band for the ceremony."

She pressed the phone to her ear. The conversation was brief. When it concluded, she sat there quietly for a moment, as though taking in what she'd learned.

He gave her a brief glance. "Well, don't just sit there. Tell me what they said."

"There's been an accident, and two of the band members have been injured."

"That's awful." He slowed to a stop at an intersection.

"I agree. Thankfully everyone lived, but they will need some time to recover. In the meantime, we don't have any music for the wedding."

"Maybe this is a sign," he said.

"A sign?"

"That the wedding shouldn't happen."

She gasped. "Are you serious? You don't think Hermione and Atlas should get married?"

He shrugged. He should have kept his thoughts to himself. When he glanced over at Adara, he found her staring expectantly at him. He focused back on the road. "What? You have to admit that nothing about this wedding is easy. The bride and groom aren't even here."

"They are where they're needed. And the wedding doesn't have to be easy. It just has to be right for Hermione and Atlas."

"If you say so."

"I do."

"So what are you going to do?"

"Me?" Her voice rose an octave. "Why should I fix this problem? I thought you wanted to help with the wedding plans. Wasn't that what you said?"

She surely didn't think he would know what to do about this latest problem. "Yes, but this is different."

"Different how?"

"Because it's an urgent problem. The wedding isn't far off."

"And why should I fix it instead of you?"

He panicked and reached for the first excuse he could think of. "Because you're a woman and this is a wedding."

When he chanced a glance in her direction, she was sitting there with her arms crossed as she glared at him. "Really? Are you saying a man can't plan a wedding?"

He sighed. "I'm certain a man could do just as good of a job planning a wedding."

"You think so?"

"I do."

"Good. Then you can find a replacement musical group."

He tapped the brakes a little too hard, jerking them in their seats. "What?"

"You heard me. Unless you don't think you're up to it."

He briefly turned to her with an arched brow

before focusing back on the road. "Is that a challenge?"

A smile tugged at the corners of her lips as she settled back in her seat. "Why, yes, it is."

He refused to back down. How hard could it be? And maybe this would at last get him back in her good graces so they could pick up where they'd left off. The thought definitely appealed to him.

There was a moment of silence as he pulled the car off on the berm of the road, and then he turned to her. "What exactly do I need to do?"

"The booking agent is going to email us a list of available musical groups."

"And then what?"

"Then you go listen to them. She's going to include where they are each playing. All you have to do it stop by and check them out."

"And that's it?" He stared at her, not believing it was that easy.

"Yes. That's it."

"Fine. I'll do it." He put the car in Drive and eased back out into traffic.

He didn't like it, but he'd do it. It really didn't sound hard. Who didn't like to listen to a bit of music? It'd be even better if Adara was listening to it with him. Hmm. He might have to plan something to get her to accompany him.

CHAPTER TEN

WHAT WAS IT with this wedding?

Adara had been involved with a lot of weddings, and she couldn't recall any having this many setbacks. It was getting so bad that for a moment she wondered if Krystof was right about this being a sign that it shouldn't take place. As soon as the thought came to her, she dismissed it.

This wedding was right for both Hermione and Atlas. They truly loved each other. And no amount of wedding dilemmas would change their devotion to one another.

Adara had just finished making arrangements for a guest's twenty-fifth wedding anniversary. A party planned for the next evening on the patio with silver and white balloons, a live band, and endless champagne. Another wonderful example of how love could endure. She refused to let Krystof's negativity get to her.

She was almost to her office when her phone

rang. She glanced at the caller ID and then pressed the phone to her ear. "Hey, Hermione. How are you doing?"

"As well as can be expected. How are things there?"

"Uh…" She entered her office and closed the door. "The resort is doing fine. No problems."

"But there is a problem. I can hear it in your voice. It's Krystof, isn't it?"

Adara sank into her chair. "He's fine. And you don't need to hear this. You have enough going on with Atlas and his father."

"I could use the distraction. So Krystof is pushing for you to get back together, isn't he?"

Adara sighed. "He wants things to go back to the way they were before I mistook his foster sister for his girlfriend in Paris."

"You did what? Oh, dear. How do you feel about that?"

Part of her was eager to feel Krystof's strong arms around her as he trailed kisses down her neck. The other part of her knew that she could easily get in too deep with him. With every detail she learned, it was easier to imagine starting a real relationship with him. And in the end, she'd be left with a broken heart.

Adara swallowed hard. "I don't want to go backward. I want a real relationship. I'm not saying we would have to get married or anything like that, but I want a commitment. I want to matter to him enough that he would go out of his way to see me often and not just when it's convenient for his schedule. I want to know that I'm the only woman in his life. Is that asking for too much?"

"No." The answer was quick and firm. "But I take it that's not what he wants."

"He wants all the fun without any strings. And that was all right for a while, but now I want more."

"I'm surprised he's sticking around and not off to a card game."

"He's been helping with the wedding."

"Helping? This is certainly surprising news. How exactly has he been helping?"

This was her chance to tell Hermione about the nightmare with the dresses. She needed to tell her now so she had time to make decisions in case her dress never showed up. It just broke her heart to pile more bad news on her friend.

"There's something I should tell you," Adara said.

"I knew there was something wrong. What is it?"

"The dresses were delivered."

"And?"

"Well, um…they weren't the right dresses."

"What? But how?"

And so Adara told her about the dress mix-up and the closing of the bridal boutique. "Krystof is helping to get the word out online about the dresses. We weren't the only one to get the wrong ones. It appears the last delivery was all mixed up. We've recovered the bridesmaid dresses and we're hoping yours will turn up soon, but I can't promise we'll get your wedding gown back in time for the ceremony."

Hermione was silent for a moment as though digesting all the information. "This is awful, but this week has shown me that in the grand scheme of things, a dress isn't what's important. In the end, it doesn't matter if I have a wedding dress or not. What matters is Atlas and me promising our hearts to each other."

Things must be bad for Hermione to be so Zen over the loss of her wedding dress. Adara's heart went out to her and Atlas. "Aw…that's so sweet. You two make the perfect couple."

They talked a little more before they ended the call. Adara was more determined than ever to make sure this wedding was the best it could be.

She had been serious.

Krystof glanced at the itinerary on his phone. Adara had forwarded a list of the musical groups and the times they would perform that week. Today he had two groups to listen to. One was performing at a school this evening. Did he even want to know how old the members of the group were?

And the other was at a gallery in the city. The gallery one he didn't mind. It was the school one that he didn't want to attend. It would remind him of his childhood. It was something he didn't want to dwell on. But he refused to let Adara down.

He had to be at the school by seven. He hoped their performance was at the beginning of the show if he hoped to make it to the gallery across the city. Even then he'd be pushing it.

He put on a white button-up. He left the top buttons undone, gave the sleeves a tug and then threw on a deep blue blazer. He wore dark jeans with loafers. It was as dressy as he got—at least without a wedding or funeral involved.

He exited the suite and headed toward the lobby. When he turned the corner, he practically ran into Adara. He reached out, grabbing her arm to help her regain her balance.

In that moment, time slowed down as his gaze met hers. He watched as her blue eyes widened in surprise. When her gaze took him in, he noticed how her pupils dilated ever so slightly. If she was anyone else, he'd say she was interested in him. But she'd made it perfectly clear that she was over him.

What was it about this woman that had him wanting her, even after she'd rejected him? He decided it was best not to delve too deeply into that subject.

"Whoa." He regretted having to let her go as his arm lowered to his side. "Where are you off to in such a hurry?"

"I was actually going to see you." She took a step back and gave his attire a quick once-over.

When her gaze once more met his, he asked, "Do you approve?"

She nodded. "You look very handsome."

A smile pulled at the corners of his lips. "Thanks." He thought of telling her that she looked beautiful but refrained. He didn't want to ruin this peaceful moment. "What did you need? I don't have much time. I have to hurry if I'm going to make it to both performances."

"Well, I was going to tell you that I'm done working for today, and if you wanted, I could tag along with you tonight."

Wait. Had he heard her correctly? She was going to spend time with him—voluntarily? He felt a surge of happiness.

And then another thought came to him. She didn't trust him. She thought he was going to let their friends down without her guidance. Well, that wasn't going to happen. He'd show her.

He decided to turn the situation around. "You can come with me as long as you don't mind a late dinner."

Her eyes widened. "Did you just blackmail me into having dinner with you?"

He let out a laugh. "I wouldn't put it that way. But I was thinking that as long as I was in Athens, I would try one of their newer restaurants."

"Oh. I see." Her gaze lowered as though she were considering whether or not this was worth her time.

"It's okay. I see you're not interested. I'll go alone." He started to walk away.

"No. I'll go."

He paused and turned to her. "Are you sure?"

She hesitated. "I am."

"Then let's be on our way. I don't want to be late and miss the first performance." He didn't wait for her response as he turned and headed for the lobby.

Once they were on the road, he chanced a glance at her with the warm rays of the setting sun lingering on her face. The beauty of the moment stole his breath away. He had to remind himself that they weren't on a date.

The ride into the city was quiet. Adara spent a great deal of that time on her phone. He wondered if something important had happened. Surely it couldn't be another problem with the wedding. Or perhaps she was just using it to avoid him.

When he pulled into a parking space near the school, he asked, "Is everything okay?"

"Um…" She typed a couple more words and pressed Send before she lifted her gaze to meet his. "Yes. Why?"

"Because you've been on your phone since we left the island. I was beginning to think you were avoiding me."

"No. Of course not. It's just with the wedding, my assistant has been filling in a lot for me. And she had some questions about the notes on my calendar."

"You like to plan out every part of your life, don't you?" He couldn't imagine what that must be like. He preferred to live on a whim and a chance.

"Yes. I try to schedule most of it."

"You never do anything spontaneously?"

A frown pulled at her glossy lips. "The last time I did something spontaneous, it didn't work out at all."

He couldn't help but wonder if she was referring to her sudden appearance at his Paris hotel suite. If only she had hung around, he could have cleared things up. He didn't like that she clung to that unfortunate event and used it to reinforce her opinion that spontaneity wasn't for her.

Just like tonight, she wanted him to think that her accompanying him was spontaneous, but he had a feeling she'd had it planned out for some time. He wanted to know what had happened in life to make her so cautious.

"We should go in," she said, drawing him from his thoughts.

"Right." While she gathered her purse, he exited the vehicle and quickly rounded the back end. And then he proceeded to open her door for her. She glanced up at him with a wide-eyed stare.

"What?" he said. "Can't a guy open the door for a lady?"

Her brows furrowed together as she stood. "A lady, huh?"

This was his cue to take things further. He stepped closer. As his gaze held hers, he reached out, gently brushing his thumb down over her cheek. He lowered his voice. "A very beautiful lady."

She didn't say a word, nor did she move away. But there was this place on her neck where her pulse beat rapidly. It matched the rapid thumping of his own heart.

He should turn away. He should focus on

why they were standing in that parking lot with the lingering rays of the sun shining down on them. And yet the reason escaped him. All he could think about was kissing her.

His gaze lowered to her mouth. Her plump lower lip shimmered. It beckoned to him, drawing him to her with a force that smothered any sense of logic. Because this kiss...he knew it would change everything.

When he drew her closer, he heard the swift intake of her breath. And then he lowered his head, claiming her lips with his own. Oh, the kiss was so much sweeter than he recalled. And she was so addictive. He couldn't imagine ever getting enough of her. He could hold her in his arms all night long if she'd let him.

She didn't move immediately. In fact, he was pretty certain she was going to slap him or at the very least pull away. He didn't know how she could fight this chemistry burning between them.

As though she suddenly surrendered to the flames of desire, her lips moved beneath his. And when his tongue traced her lips, she opened up to him. A moan swelled in the back of her throat.

Her hands rested on his chest as his wrapped around her waist, pulling her snug to him. Her curves pressed into his hard planes. He wondered if she could feel the pounding of his heart.

No other woman evoked this sort of reaction from him. No other woman had ever been such a challenge. She made him think that for once the catch would be so much better than the chase—especially with those sweet, sweet kisses.

The sound of a loud car pulling into the lot drew his attention, but nothing was going to get him to let Adara go. He worried that once their kiss ended, Adara would put the wall straight back up between them. And this time the wall would be so high he wouldn't be able to scale it.

Honk-honk.

The decision was taken out of his hands when the car wanted the empty parking spot next to his car. With the utmost reluctance, he lifted his head. Adara's eyelids fluttered open. She gazed up at him with a dazed look in her eyes.

Honk.

"We better move," she said.

He nodded and then presented his arm to her. When she glanced down at it and then sent him a questioning look, he said, "Come on. You don't want to keep them waiting."

She huffed but then proceeded to place her hand in the crook of his arm.

They walked in silence across the parking

lot. He couldn't help but notice how natural it felt. Sure, he'd had lots of women on his arm, but Adara was different. Not only was she the most beautiful woman he'd ever known, but she was also the greatest challenge. And he did love a challenge. In fact, he thrived on them.

Adara jerked his arm. "Is something wrong?"

"What?" He'd been so lost in his thoughts that he hadn't been following what she'd been saying.

She stopped walking and removed her hand from his arm. "You aren't even listening to me. What's wrong?"

So she'd felt that, huh? Apparently his thoughts had been more jolting than even he had thought. "It's nothing."

"Okay. If you won't answer that question, then answer this one. Why did you kiss me?"

His gaze lowered to her now-rosy lips, thinking how much he wanted to kiss her again. With the greatest of effort, he lifted his gaze to meet hers. "Because I needed to prove something to you."

"And what would that be?"

"That spontaneity isn't a bad thing. In fact, it can be quite enjoyable." He smiled at her. "Would you like me to show you again?"

A slight pause ensued, as though she too

were tempted to indulge in another kiss. "No. That can never happen again."

Never again? He was confused. She'd enjoyed it. Of that he was certain. So why was she continuing to put up a wall between them?

He'd explained the mix-up at his Paris hotel room. Was she expecting something more from him? Adara had known from the beginning that he didn't do commitments. But he'd been utterly and completely faithful to her since they'd met on Valentine's Day. The fact that she had been the only woman in his life all this time shocked even him.

"We're going to be late." Her voice drew him from his thoughts.

She turned and walked away. He was left to follow her. He noticed how she didn't say anything about not enjoying the kiss. In fact, he'd have sworn he heard her moan—or perhaps that had been him. The smile on his face broadened. He just might need help with all these musical auditions.

The more he thought of it, the more he liked the idea. And if he were to prove that he was awful at selecting the right music for the wedding, Adara would have no choice but to accompany him to all the performances. And then they could have some more spontaneous moments.

CHAPTER ELEVEN

HE'D KISSED HER.

That wasn't the part that worried Adara. It was the part where she'd wanted more. More kisses. More touching. More of everything from him.

Her traitorous heart had run amok when his lips had touched hers. And logic had totally abandoned her. She'd clung to a man who didn't believe in commitments or putting down roots. What had she been thinking? He was a nomad and proud of it.

So even if the unfortunate incident in Paris with his sister hadn't happened, eventually their relationship would have run its course. Just like all his other relationships. And she didn't want her heart to end up a casualty of his inability to stay in one place.

She wished the wedding was over already, but it was still several days away. They would be very long days with Krystof on the island.

And trying to avoid him was not an option, with them both participating in the wedding.

And that's why when Sunday rolled around and it was time to listen to another musical group, she seriously considered skipping it. But this would mean relying on Krystof's judgment to pick the right music for the wedding. From what she'd seen on Friday evening, he didn't take this task very seriously. He was ready to pick the first group they'd heard. And though they were good, she wasn't prepared to go with the first group without doing their due diligence. This was too important to make snap decisions.

It was with the greatest hesitation that she once more pushed off what was left of her duties that day to her assistant, who surprisingly didn't complain. And then Adara headed toward her room at the resort to change into a sundress—something more appropriate for a concert in the park.

She was tempted to go to the park in her business clothes. She didn't want Krystof to think she was making an effort to look nice for him. But she had been wearing a long-sleeved blouse due to the resort's air-conditioning. It would be really warm at the park. If she were to switch into a summer dress and sandals, she'd be a lot more comfortable.

She subdued a sigh now that she'd just talked herself into dressing for their date—erm... their outing. Because there was no way she was going to date him again. She wanted more than he would ever offer.

She wasn't getting any younger. And if she wanted to find someone to build a future with, she couldn't waste her time with a man with commitment phobia. Krystof couldn't even commit to having a home. The closest thing he had to a home was a suite at a Paris hotel. Who lived their life out of a suitcase?

It didn't take her long to change clothes, but then she decided to wear her hair down and to touch up her makeup. After all, it was hard to tell who'd they run into at the park.

Knock-knock.

"Coming." She gave her reflection one last check.

Then, with her purse in hand, she started toward the door. She briefly paused to grab the throw blanket from the end of the bed. After all, they would need something to sit on.

She opened the door, and Krystof was there leaning against the doorjamb. He gave her outfit a quick once-over. "You look beautiful."

The heat started in her chest and then worked its way to her cheeks. "Thank you."

She stepped into the hallway, pulling the door closed behind her. "Shall we go?"

"Lead the way."

She needed to get this evening over as quickly as possible—before she did something she'd later regret, like confusing this outing for a date. Her steps came quicker. She could feel Krystof keeping pace with her.

"Is this a race?" he called out from behind her. "Because I get the feeling you're trying to get away from me. If that's the case, you don't have to go this evening. I can handle it on my own."

She turned to him. "I'm fine."

"Or we could just go with the first group we heard on Friday." He arched a brow, waiting for her response.

"Are you serious?"

"Sure. Why does it matter?"

"Because this wedding has to be perfect, or at least as close to perfect as I can make it. Don't you want Atlas to be happy?"

Krystof shrugged. "I don't think Atlas is going to care about the music."

"But he will care if his bride is happy."

"I just don't get it." He resumed walking.

She fell in step with him. "Get what?"

"Why he'd even want to get married. He was

doing fine on his own. And we all know that most marriages don't last."

"Wow. I knew you weren't into commitments, but I didn't know how far your dislike for them went."

He didn't look in her direction. "I'm just speaking the truth. You can look up the statistics for yourself."

She didn't know how to counter his total disrespect for marriage and love in general. And so she remained quiet as they made their way into the city and to the park.

As Krystof pulled into a parking spot, he said, "So that's it—you're not going to speak to me the rest of the evening because I'm not in favor of marriage?"

She shifted in her seat in order to face him, and only then did she realize her mistake. This car was much too small and Krystof's shoulders were far too broad, bringing her into close contact with him. Her heart pounded so loud that it echoed in her ears.

It was only when a smile lifted the corners of his very tempting lips that it jarred her back to her senses. What she needed right now was some fresh air, preferably very far from him. But since that wasn't possible at the moment, she'd take what little bit of breathing room she could get.

And with that she turned away, opened the car door, and with the blanket draped over her arm, she alighted from the vehicle. There was already a crowd of people in the park near the stage. She wanted a spot where they could clearly see the group but far enough back that they would have space to themselves.

She picked a spot straight back from the stage, under a tree where they could spread out the blanket. "What about sitting here?"

He shrugged. "Works for me."

She meant to spread the blanket by herself, but Krystof set down the insulated bag and insisted on helping her. She didn't want him being nice to her. She wanted to wallow in her frustration with him. First, for him being against this wedding. And second, for him being opposed to commitments of any kind.

When the blanket was spread out, they sat down. Krystof pulled the insulated bag over. "Would you like to eat first?"

She really didn't have an appetite at this point, but if they were eating, it would mean they didn't have to converse with each other. "We can eat. What did you pack?"

"Me? Nothing. But the kitchen was more than willing to help with our expedition."

"Yes, the resort does excel at catering to the guests." She was very proud of the people she worked with. They went above and beyond to make the guests' visits the very best.

And so she wasn't surprised when Krystof withdrew arrangements of cheeses, vegetables and fruits. It was a lot of food. And it looked quite delicious.

Just then the music started. As a local jazz group began to play, the sounds of the keyboard filled the air with a melodious tune. Two violinists, a guitar and drums stood ready for their moment to chime in. The upbeat music immediately drew her attention. Their conversation would have to wait until later.

The concert in the park had been a nice distraction.

Now that it was over and they'd returned to the resort, Adara wasn't ready for the evening to end. They still had to get to the bottom of Krystof thinking Hermione and Atlas's wedding shouldn't take place. That had her worried.

Krystof had walked with her to her room. He hesitated at the open doorway as though not sure if he should enter or not.

Adara placed her purse on the table and then turned to him. "Aren't you coming in?"

He stepped inside and closed the door before moving to the couch to sit down. "Do you think we've found a replacement band?"

"I don't know. We have one more band to hear the day after tomorrow."

"So you aren't going to pick a favorite yet?"

She shrugged before she reached inside the fridge. "Would you like something to drink?"

"Some water."

She grabbed two waters and then joined him on the couch. After she handed him the bottle, she kicked off her shoes and curled up next to him.

She was worried about Krystof. Something from his past had damaged him to the point that she worried he'd never be able to truly let someone in to love him. If he couldn't believe love was possible for Atlas and Hermione, when everyone could see how they felt about each other, how was he supposed to believe it was possible for himself?

She twisted off the cap of her bottle and took a long, slow drink, enjoying the cold water. Ever since they'd arrived at the park, she'd wanted to ask him questions, and yet she hadn't wanted to ruin the afternoon. But she couldn't hold back the questions now. She longed to understand him better.

In a gentle voice, hoping not to evoke an argument but rather to learn why he thought the way he did, she asked, "Why do you think Hermione and Atlas don't belong together?"

He lowered the bottle of water to the table. "I didn't say they don't belong together."

Now he wanted to play word games with her, but she wasn't having any part of it. "You said you thought they shouldn't get married. So if you aren't in favor of the wedding, it means you don't think they should be together."

He turned his head, and their gazes met. "Those two things are not the same. I think they make a great couple. For now."

"For now?" She rolled around the implication of his words in her mind. "So you think they're going to break up?"

He shrugged. "Statistics prove that relationships don't make the long haul."

Irritation pumped through her veins as she sat up straighter. "What is it with you and numbers?"

He lounged back and rested his arm over the back of the couch. "Numbers are reliable. Numbers make sense."

At last, they were getting somewhere. She was starting to understand what made him tick. "And is this why you spend so much time playing cards?"

He nodded. "Cards are based on odds. Odds aren't reliable, but they are understandable."

"So you don't like relationships because they

revolve around emotions? And you think emotions aren't predictable?"

He glanced away. "I guess."

It wasn't much of an acknowledgment. She wanted to know more. She felt as though they were just scratching the surface. "Why did you agree to be the best man if you don't believe the marriage will work?"

His gaze darted to her. His brows furrowed together. "Like I'm going to turn Atlas down."

"So emotions between friends do matter to you?"

"I… I didn't say anything about emotions. But Atlas is a friend. I've known him since we were in school together. I'm not going to let him down."

His loyalty to his lifelong friend meant a lot to her. It meant that he was capable of commitment. If only he would let himself take a risk on a relationship. A risk on love.

"What are you thinking?" he asked.

Heat warmed her face as she glanced away. "I was just thinking for a man who makes his living by taking risks with cards, you aren't willing to do the same thing with your life. Why is that?"

"Maybe because my whole life has been full of unknowns and risks. Now I prefer to keep my risks at the card table only."

Her heart ached for him. And now it didn't seem like he was willing to rely on anyone. She wanted him to trust her. She wanted to prove to him that not all people walked away.

Her gaze met and held his. "You can trust me. I'm not going anywhere."

CHAPTER TWELVE

HE WANTED TO trust her.

And he did…as a friend.

Krystof found himself staring into Adara's eyes. He knew she was asking him to trust her with so much more than friendship. The thought sent an arrow of fear through his heart.

He had once staked his fortune on a high-stakes card game, and it had unnerved him much less than letting down his guard with Adara. He knew she had a way about her that could get past all his defenses. And it would be so easy to let himself care about her more than was safe.

"Tell me about it." Adara's voice was soft and coaxing. "Tell me who turned you against relationships."

He resisted the temptation to lay open all his harrowing scars. He'd never felt this compulsion before—not before he'd met Adara. His past was something he didn't share with anyone, including Atlas.

She placed her hand on his thigh. "You can talk to me—about anything. You don't have to keep putting up walls between us."

Was that what she thought he was doing? Because what he was really doing was protecting her from how messed up he really was on the inside. If she knew about his past, she would run for the door and not look back. He was nothing but damaged goods.

He lowered his arms to his sides and rubbed his damp palms over his thighs. "You don't want to know this."

"I do. If you'll share it with me."

Maybe that's exactly what he should do. He should lay it all out there for her to see that he was never going to be the traditional loving husband and devoted father she wanted. Even if he could stop moving, he wouldn't know how to be either of those things. Adara deserved someone so much better than him.

If he told her about his past, he also knew any hope of them resuming their friends-with-benefits relationship would be over. She would see through his outward facade of being successful and instead see how truly broken he was on the inside. He would once again be totally alone in this world.

It was one thing to choose this solitary life without knowing what it'd be like to share it with someone loving and caring, like Adara, but to know that sort of kindness and companionship and then to lose it—well, it might be more than he could bear. The thought of that sort of loss scared him.

And nothing scared him. He had no choice. He had to do whatever he could to dissuade Adara from wanting more from him than he could give her.

Before he could change his mind, the long-buried memories came rushing back to him. The feeling of helplessness he'd felt growing up crashed over him. And when he'd finally become a legal adult—when he was on his own—there was an unrelenting sense of determination that he was never going to feel trapped by his memories. He would tell her, and then he'd cram those haunting thoughts back in the box at the back of his mind.

Adara didn't say anything as he struggled to pull his thoughts together. He'd never stopped long enough for anyone to question his nomad lifestyle or his lack of a place to call home. In fact, he'd been doing it for so long that he'd thought of it as normal…until Adara happened into his life. Now how did he explain any of this to her?

He cleared his throat. "I never knew my parents. To this day, I don't know if they are alive or dead. I don't know their names. I don't know why they abandoned me. I don't even know what my birth name was or if I ever had one. My name was given to me by a social worker."

He chanced a glance at Adara as unshed tears gathered in her eyes. His body stiffened. He didn't want anyone's pity, most especially hers.

He refocused on his bottle of water, now sitting on the table. If he continued to take in her emotional response to his story, he didn't think he'd get through it.

But he must tell it. He had to make it clear to her why they didn't belong together—of why he couldn't transform into the man she deserved. He would do it for her. And then, when he'd bared his soul to her, he would move on, just like he'd been doing his whole life.

His mouth grew dry as his mind conjured up the painful memories. He swallowed hard. "My third, no, my fourth set of foster parents had no patience with me. I got into trouble every day of my childhood. I was curious and far too smart for my own good. By the time I was old enough to think for myself, I knew I had to get away. I didn't belong there. I believed my birth parents were out there waiting for me and I just had to find them. I was certain if that happened, everything would be right in the world."

He paused as he gathered his emotions. He

could remember the desperation he felt as a little boy, longing for the love of his parents. He'd felt so lost and alone with people who didn't like him, much less love him.

All this time, Adara sat there quietly taking it all in. He wanted to look at her, but he didn't allow himself. It was all he could do to hold it all together and get through this story—his story.

He cleared his throat. "Each time I ran away, I was returned to the home. I would be locked in a small, windowless room for days at a time. There was nothing in there. No bed. No blanket. Not even so much as a pillow. Sometimes I felt like I was going to lose it in there."

In his mind, he could still see the details of those four walls. No one should ever be treated that way. "My foster sister was the only person in that home that I ever felt close to. She would sneak over to my door when the adults were distracted. We'd play word games. I don't know if I'd have made it through that period without Celeste. I will forever be indebted to her. If she had been caught, she would have paid dearly."

Adara placed her hand on his and squeezed. "I didn't realize."

He shook his head. "Of course you wouldn't. Only Celeste knows what I went through, because she lived it with me. To this day, I still have to deal with episodes of claustrophobia." He turned to her. "Do you understand what I'm saying?"

"I'm sorry all of that happened to you. I can't even begin to understand what you lived through." Her eyes shone with sympathy.

"Don't do that. Don't look at me like that. I didn't tell you so you'd feel sorry for me. I told you so you would understand that I can never be the man you deserve."

"The man I deserve? I don't understand."

He pulled his hand away from her and stood. He began to pace. "I can't stop moving around. I can't feel trapped in a house—in a traditional life. I… I just can't do it."

He couldn't believe he'd admitted all this to her. It wasn't that he didn't trust her, because he did. He knew she'd keep the skeletons of his past to herself. But he couldn't help but wonder what she thought of him now. Did she think less of him because he wasn't able to overcome a childhood trauma? Or, worse, did she feel sorry for him?

He moved toward the door. He should leave. He'd told her about his pathetic background. He'd told her how broken he was. And now she knew that they would never be together—not in the way she wanted.

And then he felt her hands on his back. She

didn't say anything as her arms wrapped around his sides, and then her cheek pressed to his back. For a moment, she held him, and he let her. He went to remove her hands, but once he touched her, his hands stayed there. For that moment, he let himself take comfort in her touch.

As they stood there quietly, moisture dropped onto his hand. Where had it come from? And then there was another drip. He lifted his head to see if there was a leak in the ceiling. He didn't see anything.

He raised his hand to his cheek and found the moisture had come from him. They were the tears he'd never allowed himself to shed. He'd always told himself he was strong—that he didn't need to cry. But being here with Adara, all his suppressed feelings had come erupting to the surface. He was helpless to hold back the tidal wave of emotions.

When Adara let go of him, he thought she was walking away. Instead she came to stand in front of him. She gazed up at him with warmth in her eyes. She reached out and caressed his cheek, wiping away his tears.

And then she did something most unexpected. She lifted up on her tiptoes and pressed her lips to his. He hadn't known how much he needed her touch until she was kissing him.

He felt like a drowning man—a man drowning in his loneliness and self-isolation. And Adara was a life preserver pulling him back to the land of the caring.

He kissed her with a need and hunger that he'd never known before. He wrapped his arms around her waist, drawing her to him. Her soft curves fit perfectly to his hard planes. Oh, how he'd missed her.

In that moment, he didn't think about the implications of what they were about to do. There were no promises of tomorrow. There was only here and now. Living in the moment, he scooped her up in his arms. Her hands slipped around his neck.

Their kiss never stopped. It was as if she were oxygen and without her he would suffocate. He carried her to the king-size bed and gently laid her down. She wouldn't let go of him and instead pulled him down on top of her.

This was going to be a memorable night. If it was their last time together, he wanted the memories of her to carry with him forever.

CHAPTER THIRTEEN

OH, WHAT A NIGHT.

Before her eyes were even open, Adara reached out for Krystof. Her fingers touched nothing but an empty spot. Her hand moved up and down the sheet. The spot was cold.

Her eyes fluttered open. She scanned the room. There was no sign of him. He must have left sometime during the night.

That was something he never would have done before. He was always there in the morning. Granted, he was always the last one up in the morning. He claimed he was a night owl, while she was an early bird. A smile tugged at the corners of her lips at the memory.

But this morning there was no shared coffee in bed or the teasing of how he would groan that it was too early to get out of bed yet. Today he was already gone.

Even though he had slipped away while she was sleeping, she wasn't upset. In fact, she was hopeful. Last night had been a big break-through for them. She now understood him in a way she never had before.

People he was supposed to be able to trust the most in the world had let him down in the worst way. First, his birth parents had abandoned him as a toddler. And then his foster parents had abused him. Tears stung her eyes as she took it all in. How could they do such monstrous things to a child?

She was so thankful that Celeste had been there for him. Her feelings toward the woman shifted from jealousy to gratefulness. It's funny sometimes how life worked out. Maybe someday she and Celeste would be friends.

Chime.

She reached for her phone. It was a reminder for her doctor's appointment. She turned it off. Today she would see the doctor about her missing monthly. She was clinging to hope that it was something minor—something that could be fixed with a week's vacation, or at worse with some medicine.

She climbed out of bed, started the coffee machine and headed for the shower. She'd deal with the doctor first, and then she'd find Krystof. She thought he might be feeling vulnerable after his admission last night, and she wanted to assure him that everything was all right between them—in fact, it was so much better than all right.

Forty-five minutes later, showered and dressed, she headed for the door. She had to drive into the city, so she needed to get going. She didn't want to get stuck in Monday-morning traffic and miss her appointment. She opened her door and nearly ran into Krystof. He was pacing outside her door.

She stopped. "How long have you been out here?"

"I... I don't know." There were shadows under his eyes, as though he hadn't slept. "Not that long."

"Why are you pacing out here? You should have come inside."

"I didn't know if you were awake, and I didn't want to bother you. You looked so peaceful when I got out of bed."

When she went to hug him, he stepped back. She tried to tell herself that it was all right. Last night had been big for him. She knew he wasn't going to take it well in the morning light.

She lifted her phone and checked the time. If she wasn't on the road in five minutes, she was going to be late, and she just couldn't afford to miss this appointment.

"Krystof, we need to talk, but I have an important appointment right now. I can't miss it. Can we talk later?"

His gaze searched hers. And then he nodded.

She lifted up on her tiptoes and pressed a kiss to his unshaven cheek. And then she headed down the hallway. She had no idea what would come of her appointment, but she was hoping for good news. And later they'd talk. Everything was going to work out.

She'd blown him off.

She didn't see him the same way she used to.

Krystof needed something to keep his mind from the ghosts of the past, the mess of the present and the impossibility of the future. His gut reaction was to hop on his plane and jet off to the next big card game. It's what he did when life got too complicated.

And yet he'd promised Adara he'd be here to help her with the wedding. He didn't want to break his word to her, even if staying here and facing the sympathy in her eyes would be one of the hardest things he had ever done.

He had his assistant send over the financials for the tech company he was seriously considering buying. It would give him the ability to expand MyPost into a more varied social media platform—so it could help people the way he'd been using it to help reunite brides with their missing wedding gowns. As of this morning, there were five relieved brides, but there was still no sign of Hermione's wedding dress. But he wasn't giving up hope.

As he pulled up the financial statements and various spreadsheets on his laptop, he started to relax. Numbers were reliable. They never lied. They were always what they appeared. One plus one always equaled two.

Minutes turned to hours as he worked in his suite, closing out the rest of the world. He shoved thoughts of Adara and all that had happened the previous evening to the back of his mind—even memories of their lovemaking. He wasn't sure if she'd spent the night with him because she'd truly wanted to or if she'd done it out of sympathy. He had the feeling it was the latter, and that made him feel even worse.

Come that evening, there was an alert on his phone. Thinking it was from his assistant, he checked it. To his surprise, there was a response to his posting about the wedding dress on MyPost. Someone had Hermione's wedding dress. It wasn't for certain, but this time the pictures looked like it was the right one. In turn, it was believed that Adara had the missing dresses for their wedding party. They would be at the resort the next morning to exchange the dresses.

Krystof tried to phone Adara, but she didn't answer. He got up to get himself a cup of coffee. And then he tried again. It went to voice mail.

A frown pulled at his face. It felt as though she was avoiding him. He now suspected that she'd spent the night in his arms because she felt sorry for him. He never should have said anything to her. Instead of clarifying things, his revelation had only made everything feel so much more complicated.

He set off for her office, but when he reached it, the door was closed and locked. Next he tried her room, but she didn't answer the door. Finally he tracked down Adara's assistant. Demi checked and told him that Adara was in the penthouse. What was she doing there?

With some instructions, he made his way to the private elevator to the penthouse. He pressed the call button and wondered if Atlas and Hermione had returned. But it was Adara's voice on the intercom.

"Yes?"

He cleared his throat. "I have news."

"Come on up."

Immediately the elevator opened, and he stepped inside. He wondered what Adara was doing there. The elevator moved swiftly, and soon the door slid open. He stepped out and found Adara standing there. She looked expectantly at him.

"I've been trying to reach you," he said.

"You have?" She pulled her phone from her

pocket, glanced at the screen and then frowned. "It died. I forgot to charge it last night."

He was the reason she'd forgotten. "About last night—"

"Why don't you come in? Indigo is here." She turned and headed for the living room of Hermione and Atlas's home.

He followed her. His gaze moved around, taking in all the wedding supplies. And then his attention focused on Indigo, who was sitting at a table near one of the floor-to-ceiling windows that offered the most amazing view of the sea. Greetings were exchanged.

He turned to Adara. "What's going on?"

She sat down at the table. "We're working on the final details. And you're just in time to help."

He shook his head. "I don't think so."

"Oh, come on." Indigo patted the chair next to her.

He hesitated, but he didn't want to be rude, so he finally sat down. "What are you doing?"

"These are *koufeta*." Adara held up a white tulle pouch of sugar-coated almonds.

He watched as she gave the tulle a twist and added white ribbon with a small printed note with the wedding date as well as the bride and groom's names.

"Why are you wrapping nuts?" He could honestly admit that he knew nothing about wedding traditions.

"The almond symbolizes endurance." Indigo added almonds to a piece of tulle and gave it a twist.

"And the sugar coating symbolizes a sweet life." Adara finished tying a bow and adjusting the note before setting the favor aside. "See, it's easy. Now wash up." When he hesitated, Adara said, "Hurry. We have two hundred favors to make."

"Two hundred?" Surely he hadn't heard her clearly.

She nodded. "They wanted to include as many friends and resort employees as they could, since neither of them have much family. Now go."

He reluctantly got up and moved to the kitchen, where he washed his hands. He did notice that Adara wasn't acting any different than normal with him. Was it possible that she'd gotten over whatever had had her rushing off this morning? He hoped so.

When he returned to the table, he noticed a stack of cut tulle at his spot as well as a bowl of almonds. He supposed he could help for a little bit. After all, two hundred was a lot of favors to put together.

Both Adara and Indigo were busy adding almonds to their tulle. He spooned some almonds into his piece of material.

He was just about to give the tulle a twist when Adara asked, "Did you count the number of *koufeta*?"

He shook his head. "I didn't know I was supposed to."

"You have to," Indigo said. "The number of *koufeta* needs to be odd, because an odd number is undividable. It symbolizes the bride and groom will remain undivided."

It made sense, he supposed. He did like the part that relied upon numbers. And so he set to work. Adara made a couple of adjustments to his first favor. By his fifth one, he was on his own.

"So why did you need to see me?" Adara asked.

And then he realized he hadn't told her about the reason for him stopping by. "The wedding dress has been found."

"What?" Adara stopped what she was doing to look at him with her mouth gaping. "Really?"

He nodded and smiled. He was so glad he was able to make her happy again. "They're bringing it to the resort tomorrow."

"That's amazing," Indigo said. "You're a lifesaver. Just wait until Hermione hears the news."

"Hermione." Adara jumped up. "I have to call her." She reached for her phone but then put it back on the table. "But my phone is dead."

He pulled his out of his back pocket and held it out to her. "Here. Use mine."

"Thanks. Hermione's going to be so relieved." Adara moved to the balcony to place the call.

With some wine, they continued to work. Dinner was delivered to the penthouse. Krystof eventually gave up on trying to slip away. Because not only did they have favors to assemble, but they also had some table decorations to make. By the time they finished, it was close to midnight, and they were all exhausted.

Tired or not, Krystof was relieved. Things were mostly back to normal with Adara. Granted, she was a little more quiet than usual, but he'd told himself that she was tired. And why wouldn't she be? She was always working. Maybe he should do something about that.

CHAPTER FOURTEEN

SHE DIDN'T DO well with waiting.

Instead she threw herself into her work.

Tuesday morning, Adara sat behind her desk. She had just finished setting up a surprise engagement for one of the resort's regular guests. They were planning to have a plane fly over the beach with a banner that read, Will You Marry Me? Adara smiled at the thought. It was certainly a grand gesture.

Krystof stepped through her open doorway. "Are you ready?"

She blinked and looked at him. "Ready for what?"

"Remember, the dress is being dropped off today." He arched a brow. "I can't believe you'd forget something like that."

"Sorry. I've just had a lot on my mind lately." That was the biggest understatement of her life. In that moment she realized she'd been so caught up in her medical drama, she'd never had that talk with Krystof. "I'm sorry I got distracted and we never got to talk."

"No problem." He sent her a smile that didn't quite reach his eyes. "What has you so worried?"

Could he read her so easily? She hoped not. "The…uh…wedding, of course. There's just so many details. And we have to confirm a replacement musical group for the ceremony."

"I was thinking about that, and I already have a favorite."

"But you haven't heard the last one yet."

"I don't need to hear them. I already like this one."

She sighed. Normally she'd insist on hearing the final group, but time was short. "Okay. If we agree on the same musical group, then we'll skip the party tonight. Agreed?"

"Agreed."

"Then what group did you like?"

"I liked the string quartet at the school. They were excellent and classy."

Her mouth gaped. They'd just agreed on something. "I was just thinking the same thing. I'll call the booking agent and set it up. One less thing to worry about."

"Now let's go get those dresses," he said.

She glanced down at her desk and the other things that needed her attention. A busy resort meant there were a lot of guests with a lot of requests.

"Come on," Krystof said. "That can all wait."

"Easy for you to say. You don't have to deal with any of it."

With a sigh, she stood. They went to meet the woman and her daughter. The gowns were exchanged and then Hermione's wedding dress was placed in the penthouse for safekeeping. After so much worry, it was such an easy, painless resolution.

"I'm so relieved," Adara said on the elevator ride down to the main floor.

"Now you can stop worrying so much."

"Not yet—there's still a lot to do before they say 'I do.'"

"What you need is a nice, relaxing lunch."

She glanced at the time on her phone. "It's not even noon yet."

"It will be soon. And I have something special in mind."

"Krystof, you don't understand. I have a meeting at one with Mr. Grant. And I have a meeting at two with the Papadopouloses."

"What I have to show you is more important."

Concern came over her. "What is it? What's wrong? Does it have something to do with the wedding?"

"Just come with me." He gave her outfit a once-over. "Do you have something more casual to wear?"

"Not with me. I didn't anticipate needing anything casual."

"No worries. We'll take care of it." He took her hand in his. "Come with me."

"But my appointments—"

"No worries. May I borrow your phone?"

"No." She tightened her hold on her phone. Without it, she'd be lost. It had her calendar and all her contacts. "Why do you want it?"

"Never mind." He turned to the left and walked toward her assistant, Demi.

What in the world had gotten into him? He'd been acting different ever since he'd told her about his past the other night. And he was certainly intent on showing her something today.

Part of her wanted to run off with him. The other part of her said that she had responsibilities here at the resort. She was torn as to what she should do. Finally the curiosity about what had him so excited won over. What was he up to?

Where was the fun in her life?

She worked all the time.

Krystof knew he might not be serious and responsible—at least by other people's estimations of him—but he had a different outlook on life. If you took it too seriously, it would do you in.

He'd promised himself that he would enjoy his life. He wouldn't get hung up with the normal responsibilities that people sometimes found themselves trapped in. And so when he'd found that he had a knack for cards, he'd used it to his advantage. After all, who could turn down a challenge? Because that's what a poker game came down to—who could outbluff who?

But Adara was so locked into her routine that her life lacked any real moments of fun and spontaneity. Maybe if she were to experience some with him, she would understand him better.

After a stop at the boutique for some casual clothes and swimsuits followed by a visit to the Cabana Café, he took her hand and they set off on their journey. This outing would do them both some good. They'd been too intense about this wedding and other things. They needed to remember how to have fun.

"Where are we going?" she asked. "I thought maybe we were going on a boat ride, but you're leading us away from the water."

The vegetation grew denser. The leafy trees, lush greenery and bright flowers were beautiful, with shades of green and pinks and reds lining the dirt path. He noticed how Adara slowed down to smell the wildflowers.

When the trees grew denser, it provided a canopy. Slices of sunlight made it through here and there, lighting up the ground. He had never been to a more beautiful place. The gentle sea breeze rustled through the trees' leaves and carried with it a light floral scent.

"It's beautiful out here," Adara said.

"You make it sound like you've never been here before."

"I haven't."

"What?" He stopped in front of her. "You mean to tell me you've been working at the resort for years and you never ventured outside?"

She shrugged. "What? Don't look at me like that. It's not like I was a guest. I was hired to work here. And that's what I do."

"And you never wanted to escape your office to go explore the island?"

"I didn't say that. But I can't just run off whenever I feel like it. I have people counting on me to do my job. Not everyone can be like you."

Ouch. Her comment zinged right into his chest with a wallop. Maybe she was right. Maybe he should take on more responsibility. He thought of that tech company in Paris. He'd gone through the financials and didn't see any reason he shouldn't buy it.

"I'm sorry," she said apologetically. "I shouldn't have said that. I know it's the only life you know. The only life you want."

He paused and stared into her eyes. It wasn't the only life he knew. Because of her, he was finding there was more to life than he'd allowed himself to experience. And there were definite benefits to staying in one place.

"Come on. We're almost there." At least he hoped so. He'd heard about this spot from Titus, the front desk clerk.

They continued to walk until the trees grew sparse and the sound of water could be heard in the distance.

Her face lit up. "Is that the waterfall?"

"If my directions are correct, then yes. That's the twin falls."

With her hand still in his, she took off in a rush. They moved quickly over the overgrown path. It didn't appear many of the guests ventured far from the beach to experience this raw beauty.

Adara didn't stop until they had a clear vision of the twin falls—a high waterfall that spilled onto a piece of rock that jutted out and then a much shorter waterfall that ran into a pond down below.

He moved to a clearing, where he spread out a blanket and placed the picnic basket next to it. The bright sunshine rained down on them. This had to be one of the most magnificent places in the world, but its beauty couldn't compare to Adara's.

He watched as she turned around in a circle, taking in the scenery. The smile on her face told him everything he needed to know. His surprise pleased her.

While she looked around, he stepped off to the side and plucked a white orchid. With the bloom held behind his back, he approached Adara. "I take it you've never been here, either?"

"No. Never. It's so peaceful and beautiful."

He stepped closer to her and held out the orchid. "Not nearly as beautiful as you."

Color flooded her cheeks. She accepted the flower. "Thank you."

His gaze met and held hers. His heart started to pound. All he wanted to do in that moment was to draw her into his arms and hold her close, but he resisted the urge.

"I brought you here," he said, "because I wanted to show you that spontaneity can be good, too. Your whole life doesn't have to be planned out. Leave some room for the unexpected."

"I'm starting to think you might have a good point."

A smile pulled at his lips. "I'm glad. Now, let's have some fun."

When he pulled off his polo shirt and tossed it on the ground, her eyes grew round. "Krystof, I like the way you think." She glanced around. "But not here. What if someone saw us?"

He let out a laugh and pulled her to him. He pressed a kiss to her lips. "I like the way *you* think. But you don't have to worry."

Disappointment flickered across her face. "So you didn't bring me out here to seduce me?"

"I didn't say that. But that will have to wait for a moment." He enjoyed the way her cheeks turned pink at the thought of their lovemaking. "I have something else in mind first." He took off his socks and shoes. He glanced over at her. "You might not want to wear all of that."

She arched a brow. "You just want to see me in my new bikini, don't you?"

"Well, of course." He placed his socks in his shoes.

He told himself that he should turn away. If he got distracted, he'd forget the reason he'd brought her out here. But then her gaze met his and she gave him a mischievous grin. She gently placed the orchid on the ground next to her. When she straightened, she pulled out the hem of her blouse from her shorts.

His breathing changed to shallow, rapid breaths. And then she slowly unbuttoned her shirt. His heart beat frantically. This was the sweetest torture he'd even endured. His gaze was glued to her. There was no chance of him turning away. His body simply refused to move.

And then, ever so slowly, the shirt slid off her slim shoulders before fluttering to the ground. The breath caught in his throat. He should do something. Say something. But he continued to stand there as if in a trance.

When she reached for her shorts, he thought his heart was going to beat out of his chest. She undid the button on her waistband. He swallowed hard. She slowly unzipped them. She wiggled her hips, allowing the shorts to slip down, and then she stepped out of them. His mouth went dry as he took in the little yellow bikini from the resort boutique that showed off her curves.

"Do you like what you see?" Her voice was deep and sultry.

His voice didn't work, so he vigorously nodded.

She stepped up to him, lifted up on her tiptoes and pressed her lips to his. He kissed her back. He'd never tire of having her so close.

There was something so very special about her—something he needed in his life.

When he went to pull her closer, she quickly backed away. A smile played upon her lips. "You said you brought me all the way out here for something other than kissing, so what did you have in mind?"

He sighed. "Did you have to throw my words back in my face?"

A big smile lit up her eyes, making them twinkle. "Yes, I did."

He took her hand in his. "Okay. Let's go."

He led her toward the lower waterfall. There was a large space between the two layers of rock. He led her to that protected area. While they were shielded from the rushing water, in front of them the waterfall flowed down from above, hitting the layer of rock they stood on, and then the water spilled down into the pond below.

"This is so amazing." Adara practically had to shout to be heard over the waterfall.

He turned to her. "Almost as amazing as you."

When she looked at him like he was the only man in the world, his resolve crumbled. He drew her into his arms. And as they stood there on the rocks with the water spilling down, he claimed her lips with his own.

He was finding that the more time he spent

with her, the more time he wanted to spend with her. And his driving need to keep moving around—to never stay in one place too long—was dissipating.

With the greatest regret, he pulled back. If they were to kiss any longer, his reason for bringing her out here would be lost. He took her hand in his as he made his way to the edge of the rock.

Adara stopped. "What are you doing?"

He turned to her. "Come on."

"Out there?" She pointed to the edge. "I don't think so."

"You can do it."

"And what are we going to do once we get out there?"

"We're going to jump?"

"Jump!" She started shaking her head. "No. Not a chance."

He gave her hand a reassuring squeeze. "It'll be fun."

"You don't even know if it's safe. What if the water down below is too shallow?"

"I'll have you know I asked Titus at the front desk about it. He said this is a popular cliff-jumping spot. Don't you trust me?"

"I… I trust you." Her gaze moved to follow the water down to the pond below.

"Then come on. Do something spontaneous."

"I did. I came here with you."

"Yes, you did." His thumb moved back and forth over the back of her hand. "Now let's go do something daring."

Her skeptical gaze met his. "You're serious, aren't you?"

"Of course I am." He kept a hold on her hand as he continued toward the edge.

She hesitated at first, but then she followed him. "I can't believe you want us to jump off a cliff."

"It's not a very high one."

Her gaze lowered to the water down below. "High enough."

He turned to her. "Will you jump with me?"

"I… I don't know."

She was so close. He just needed to coax her a little more out of her comfort zone. And then he hoped it would be the first of many new experiences for them.

"What will it take to convince you to jump with me?"

She cautiously leaned forward to peer at the water below, and then she pulled back. "I get to pick our next date."

He liked the idea of there being a promise of another date. "I'll do whatever you want."

"Then what are you waiting for?"

Hand in hand, they moved to the edge of the

cliff. He turned his head to look at her. She gazed into his eyes. This was a new beginning for them.

Her heart raced as the blood pulsated in her ears. Adara chanced a glance to the side, at the water rushing down to the pond below. He really wanted them to jump? All the way down there?

Krystof squeezed her hand. When she glanced back at him, he said, "You don't have to do this if you really don't want to."

She swallowed hard. "I know."

Part of her wanted to turn and go back to the place where they'd left their picnic lunch. It would be the safe thing to do—the smart thing to do. And yet her feet wouldn't move.

As she stared into his eyes, it calmed her. She instinctively knew he would never do anything to endanger her. All he wanted her to do was to step outside her comfort zone. But could she do it?

It was so far down there. She had never done something like this before. Maybe this wasn't the best way to step out of her comfort zone. Maybe she should find some other thing to do. Yes, that sounded like a good idea.

"Adara, you can do this. You'll be with me." Krystof's voice was deep and soothing.

"Couldn't we go back down and have a picnic lunch?"

"We will, soon. I promise." He held his hand out to her.

She glanced down at the water again. She turned her head back to him. Her attention focused on his outstretched hand. Her heart pounded in her chest as she placed her hand in his. Her fingers laced with his as though it were the most natural thing.

Don't back out. You can do this.

She needed to prove to herself that she could do the daring and unexpected. Maybe since her parents' deaths, she had sought safety and security within her scheduled plans. Maybe now, with so much time having passed, it was finally time to try something different.

Her gaze rose to his. "Let's do this."

He smiled at her and then nodded. "Let's." They both turned to the edge of the cliff. "At the count of three."

By now she was clutching his hand so tight that it must be cutting off his blood flow, but he didn't complain. Had she forgotten to tell him that she didn't like heights?

"One…"

Her heart beat against her ribs.

"Two…"

Why did it look so far down?

"Three…"

The jerk of his hand spurred her into action. And then she felt weightless as she fell.

Splash.

Somewhere along the way, she'd lost hold of Krystof. She sank deep into the water. She felt as though she were never going to stop slipping farther into the dark depths of the pond.

At long last her body stopped dropping. Now she had to get to the surface. She started to kick her legs, hoping she was headed in the right direction. It was hard to tell as the light moved through the water. She hoped she was swimming upward.

She kicked hard. Her lungs began to burn. She kicked harder. Where was the surface? Panic had her swimming with all her might. Was she almost there?

And then she broke the surface. She gulped down oxygen, never so happy to be able to breathe. She coughed, having inhaled a little water.

"Are you okay?" Krystof's voice came from behind her.

She gathered herself and turned in the water to face him. He was smiling at her. "What are you smiling about?"

"You did it. You took a chance and did something out of the ordinary."

And then she realized he was right. She beamed back at him. "I did. Thanks to you."

She swam closer to him and wrapped her arms around his neck. He lowered his head and caught her lips with his own. His skin was chilled from the water, but she didn't mind, because his touch was all she needed to warm her up.

As their kiss intensified, her legs encircled his waist. The temperature of the water was long forgotten. She had other, more urgent matters on her mind now.

With her wrapped in his arms, Krystof swam on his back to the edge of the pond. He released her to heft himself out first, and then he turned back to help her out.

He swept her up into his arms and resumed kissing her. He carried her back to the clearing. He gently laid her down on the blanket. She refused to let him go. She drew him down on top of her. For her, this was the greatest risk of all. Because every time they made love, he made his way deeper into her heart.

CHAPTER FIFTEEN

LIFE COULD CHANGE in the time it took to flip a coin.

Adara should know, since it'd just happened to her.

One moment, she felt as though her feet were floating above the ground. She'd been so proud of herself for cliff jumping. It was something she'd never done before. It showed her that she could accomplish things she hadn't even considered until this point.

Throughout their picnic lunch at the waterfall followed by their dinner in bed, as well as the following two days they'd spent together, she had started to envision her life a bit differently. She'd even considered what she might do if she no longer worked at the Ludus Resort. After all, her assistant, Demi, was a natural. She could take over, and Adara would be free to do something else. The problem was that she liked her work as a concierge. She liked working with people and making their visions come true.

Krystof pushed her to question her life's decisions. Had she settled too soon? Should she have explored the world more to see if there was somewhere else that she fit in? Should she have worried more about her romantic life than her career? If she'd focused on romance, maybe she'd already have a baby and her current medical problem wouldn't feel so enormous.

The doctor's office had called on Friday morning and insisted they couldn't give her the test results over the phone. She had to meet with the doctor. It was at this point that she could no longer pretend this situation wasn't serious. They never called you into the office to give you good news.

It was the worst time, too. Atlas and Hermione had just arrived back on the island. With the wedding taking place tomorrow, they needed to finish up some last-minute wedding details. However, Adara couldn't delay her doctor's visit. She needed to know what was going on with her. She'd quietly slipped away.

The doctor had told her she was having early-onset menopause. She'd replayed his words over and over in her mind. How was this possible? She was only thirty-two. No one she knew went through menopause that early.

When he'd mentioned that sometimes it ran in families, she'd thought of her mother. Adara had been their only child. Whenever she'd asked her mother for a little brother or sister, her mother had said that wasn't going to happen. Maybe now Adara understood why her mother had looked so sad when she'd said those words.

And now Adara's vision for the future was ruined. There would be no happy little family for her. She wouldn't know what it was like to carry a baby in her body. She wouldn't hold her baby in her arms. Each time the thoughts tormented her, the backs of her eyes stung with unshed tears. She blinked them away. They would have to wait. She didn't have time to mourn the future she'd envisioned.

Right now, they'd just finished an elaborate wedding rehearsal dinner. The six members of the wedding party had dined out on the penthouse balcony. She'd love to say the food was delicious, but she hadn't eaten much, and what she had eaten had tasted like cardboard.

While Krystof, Atlas and Istvan were inside getting everyone some more drinks, the women were seated at the table. Hermione was all smiles. She looked like the happiest bride.

"How is Atlas's father doing?" Adara asked her friend.

"He's been moved to physical rehab. I was

hoping he could be here for the wedding, but everyone agreed it would be too much for him."

"I'm sorry he couldn't make it," Indigo said. "But we'll take lots of pictures for you to share with him."

"Thank you. I think he'd like that. He's changed a lot since Atlas last saw him," Hermione said. "He's been sober for three years now. He apologized to Atlas. And I think he really meant it."

"How did Atlas feel about that?" Adara asked.

"He's being cautious. And I can't blame him after all he's been through. But I think there's a chance for some sort of relationship going forward. I just don't know what it'll look like. I guess it's just going to be a day-by-day thing." Hermione turned to Adara. "And how are things with you and Krystof? I hear you two have been spending a lot of time together."

Adara hesitated. She wasn't ready to dissect her complicated relationship with Krystof. Yesterday she would have said they were both learning to take risks and they might have a chance at building a lasting relationship. But today, after speaking to the doctor, she felt confused and unsure about what her future would hold.

Hermione didn't need to know any of this at her rehearsal dinner. Adara frantically searched for a more neutral topic of conversation.

Indigo leaned forward. "On Tuesday, they went cliff jumping at the twin falls."

"What?" Hermione's eyes opened wide. "But why?"

Adara shrugged. "Why not?"

Hermione smiled and shook her head. "Looks like Krystof is having an influence on you. If I'm not careful, he'll steal you away from me."

Adara shook her head. "I don't think so. What would I do? I couldn't just follow him around the world watching him play cards."

"I'm sure you could find something much more entertaining to do with him." Indigo laughed.

As Adara's face grew warm, Hermione let out a giggle.

"What's going on out here?" Atlas handed Hermione a drink.

"We were just catching up on things." Hermione thanked her fiancé and then sipped at her drink.

Krystof placed a hand on Adara's bare shoulder. His touch felt good. She resisted the urge to lean her head against his arm. She refused to allow herself even that small bit of comfort. The news from the doctor had her seeing things differently—had her pulling back from Krystof.

With his other hand, Krystof handed her some ice water. They'd cut off the bubbly a while ago, because no one wanted to party too much with the wedding tomorrow.

He crouched down next to her. "Can I get you anything else?"

She shook her head. "I'm good."

He'd never been this sweet and attentive before. He was changing before her eyes. She didn't know what it meant, but she definitely felt like he was moving in the right direction. The destination was still a bit fuzzy, though.

The wedding day had arrived.

With the sun barely above the horizon, Adara was wide-awake and showered. She was a mixture of excited and relieved. She couldn't believe all the obstacles they'd had to overcome to make it to this point.

Ding.

She reached for her phone resting next to the bed. It was probably Hermione thinking of one last detail for the wedding. But when she read the message, she learned it was the bakery delivering the cake. *This early?*

She texted back that she would be right there. She twisted her hair and clipped it up. Later she would do something more formal for the wedding. Right now, she had to make sure the cake made it safely into the walk-in fridge.

In a pink flowered summer dress and sandals, she rushed to the elevator and down to the main floor. She hurried to the employee entrance and found the catering van. There were two deliverymen.

"Thanks for being here so early," Adara said. "This is one less thing I have to worry about."

"Where do you want these?" The shorter of the two men loaded the cake boxes onto a cart.

She explained the directions to the appropriate kitchen. "You can place the boxes on the large table to the left of the door. I'll make sure they are placed in the fridge."

The shorter man took off for the door. When she went to follow him, the taller man stopped her. "I just need you to sign off on the delivery."

"Oh. Certainly." She wondered if she should get the bride to do this, but she suspected Hermione was still tired from her journey yesterday. It was best to let her sleep as long as she could. Adara held her hand out for the receipt.

When he handed over the clipboard, she glanced at the name. Nikolaou.

Please don't let this be another mix-up.

"Um…this is the wrong bill. This is the Kappas or Othonos wedding."

The man's bushy brows drew together. "I

don't understand. This was the receipt I was given. Let me look up front." He strode to the front of the truck and swung open the door.

It took a few minutes for him to come back with a small stack of receipts. "What did you say the name was?"

She repeated the names. It took him a moment to sort through the papers. And then he pulled out a slip. "Here it is." He held it out to her. "Just sign."

She wasn't going to just sign. After the last mix-up, she didn't trust the receipt was correct. "What about the cakes? Are they the right ones?"

The man's brows scrunched together again. "Of course they're right."

She was understandably having a problem taking it for granted that the cake hadn't been mixed up just like the receipt. "Maybe I should go check."

"Lady, I don't have all day. It's the right cake. Just sign the receipt."

She crossed her arms. "How can you be sure? You mixed up the receipts."

He expelled a frustrated sigh. "Because the cakes were double-checked at the bakery and marked one through five. This is the only five-tier cake we're delivering today. Therefore it's the right cake."

His explanation sounded reasonable. While the man grumbled about falling behind in his schedule, she read down line by line. And when she was satisfied that it was correct, she signed off. He pulled off a yellow carbon copy and handed it to her.

On her way to the kitchen, she passed the shorter man with an empty cart. Now all she had to do was put the layers of cake in the fridge until it was time for the wedding, and then the kitchen crew would see to assembling it for the reception.

She smiled as she made her way through the hotel. She approached an older woman pushing her cleaning supply cart. "Good morning, Irene."

The woman sent her a big, friendly smile. "It's a gorgeous day for a wedding."

"Yes, it is. I hope you're ready to dance the evening away."

"I still can't believe they invited the staff."

"I can. Hermione looks on all of us as her family. And Atlas finally has the family he never had growing up."

Irene placed a hand over her heart as she sighed. "It's so good they found each other."

"Agreed. I have to get going and see to the cake."

"I bet it'll be beautiful."

"It will be. Soon, you'll see for yourself."

"Then I better get my work done early. I don't want to miss this wedding."

"See you later."

And then they continued in opposite directions. Irene wasn't the only excited member of staff. In fact, there had been a lottery to see which staff got to attend the wedding and which had to work, because without the lottery, it had been chaos with everyone trying to swap shifts. At last, it was settled. Some employees would be wedding guests, and the others would get a bonus in their next paycheck. It wasn't perfect, but Hermione and Atlas had done their best.

Adara entered the kitchen and looked to the left. The table was empty. Her chest tightened in panic. Where was the cake?

Her gaze swung around the kitchen, searching for the pink bakery boxes. And then she spotted them on the table to the right of the door. She blew out a pent-up breath. It appeared the guy wasn't any better with directions than the driver had been with finding the right receipt.

Adara couldn't believe how much cake there was, but Hermione had fallen in love with this design. There were alternating flavors—the bottom tier was chocolate with a cherry ganache filling, and the next layer was vanilla with a lemon curd filling. Adara's mouth watered just thinking about eating it. She wasn't sure which layer she preferred more.

Now she had to get the cake moved into the large walk-in fridge. The wedding wasn't until that afternoon, but the cooking staff would be there shortly to begin the preparations. Adara hoped to be gone before they showed up.

She walked to the fridge and stepped inside. There were mounds of food everywhere. There was a spare shelf here and there, but no group of shelves. Some rearranging was in order.

Minutes later, she had a spot for the cake boxes. She moved them one by one, starting with the largest. She held the boxes tightly and took slow, measured steps so as not to trip. She had never been so nervous while holding a cake before. But this wasn't just any cake—it was her best friend's wedding cake.

The first four layers were secure in the fridge. This just left the cake top. She couldn't resist taking a peek. She loosened the tape very carefully. She lifted the lid.

Inside was a pale blue cake with an array of pastel flowers. It was beautiful. And it would totally fit the beach theme of the wedding.

She closed the box, resealing the tape. You couldn't even tell that she'd taken a sneak peek.

She carefully lifted the box so as not to tip it to one side or the other.

With the box secure in her hands, she started across the kitchen to the fridge. Just as she stepped in front of the kitchen door, it began to open. It was as if time slowed down.

She froze. The door moved. Her voice caught in her throat.

The door hit the box. It jarred her, and she screamed, "Stop!"

CHAPTER SIXTEEN

IT WAS TOO LATE.

The door struck Adara's fingers.

It pushed her hands back. The box hit her chest. Adara gasped.

The cake box tilted. The lid pressed against her. "Oh, no! No! No! No!"

When the door moved back, she lowered the cake box. Her sole focus was on the cake inside. Was it salvageable? She doubted it.

"What's wrong?" Suddenly Krystof appeared in front of her.

"How could you?" Of all the people to be on the other side of the door, why was she not surprised to find it was Krystof? He was always acting first and thinking later.

His dark brows furrowed together. "What did I do?"

"You ruined everything!" She moved to the closest table and placed the box on it.

"Ruined everything? Don't you think that's a little overdramatic?"

"No. I don't." Her fingers shook with nervous energy as she worked to loosen the tape on the lid. "It just can't be ruined."

"What?" Frustration rang out in his voice.

Her gaze met his as she gestured at the cake box. "What do you think?"

"How am I supposed to know? Someone told me they saw you come down here, and I came to see if you needed any help."

She shook her head. "You have the worst timing ever."

His eyes widened. "Why are you so mad at me?"

All her pent-up emotions came bubbling to the surface. Instead of dealing with her infertility issues, her anger and frustration was focused on the fate of the cake.

"It doesn't matter." She didn't have time to get into this with him. "Just go."

"I'm not leaving." He moved up next to her. "What has you so upset?"

At last she managed to loosen the tape. She lifted the lid. And the cake was even worse than she'd imagined. The frosting was smashed against the lid and the side of the box. The fluffy chocolate cake was split open. Now what was she going to do?

Krystof peered over her shoulder. "Wait. Is that the wedding cake?"

"It was."

"Was?"

"You squashed it against me when you came flying through the door. How could you do that?"

"Wait." He pressed his hand to his chest indignantly. "You're blaming me?"

"Of course I am. You're the one who slammed the door into the cake."

"How was I supposed to know you were standing there? It's not like there's a window in the door or anything!"

She hated that he had a good point. Right now, she needed someplace to focus her frustration. And Krystof was the only one in the vicinity. And it might have had something to do with him trying to win her over when she knew that soon he'd be gone on his next adventure, while she'd still be here on Ludus Island. But she refused to think about that now. She had a cake disaster to deal with.

"What are you going to do?" Krystof looked at her expectantly.

She was tired of solving problems. "What are *you* going to do? After all, you are the best man. So what's it going to be? And don't take long, because we don't have much time."

His brows furrowed together. "Why should I fix it?"

"Because you ruined the cake." She sighed. There was no time for him to figure out a solution. "Never mind. I've got this." She withdrew her phone from her pocket and pulled the receipt from her pocket. She dialed the number for the bakery.

"What are you doing?"

As the phone rang, she held up her finger for Krystof to wait. After a much-too-brief conversation with the bakery, she disconnected the call.

"What did they say?" Krystof leaned against the table.

She placed her palms on the cold metal of the tabletop and leaned her weight on them as she stared straight ahead. "They can't help us. They said they delivered unblemished cakes and what happened to them after they were delivered is our problem."

"Can't they make us a new cake? I'm willing to pay whatever it'll cost. I'll even throw in a bonus."

She was relieved he was finally comprehending the severity of this situation. "They said they're fully booked today. And even if they wanted to help, there simply isn't enough time to bake a new cake, cool it, decorate it and deliver it."

Krystof raked his fingers through his hair, scattering the loose curls. "Then there won't be a cake top. There will still be a cake. That's all that's needed."

"What?" Surely she hadn't heard him correctly. "You can't be serious." When he nodded, she said, "How many weddings have you been to where there wasn't a beautifully decorated cake? And the cake top is the showpiece."

"I don't go to many weddings."

"You're avoiding the question."

He sighed. "Fine. What are you going to do?"

"I think you mean what are *we* going to do, because this mess is as much your fault as mine." Her mind raced, searching for a solution. Because she wasn't going to let Hermione down. "Let me get the next smallest cake."

"*I'll* get the cake. We know what happened the last time you carried one of the cakes."

"Hey, that's not fair."

"But true."

She inwardly groaned. "Fine. The cakes are in the walk-in. They're on the left side in pink boxes. Make sure you grab the smallest box, and please be careful. We can't afford to lose another layer."

"Trust me. I'm sure on my feet."

She rolled her eyes as he walked away. Lucky for her, she'd taken some cake-decorating classes with her neighbor. And here she'd thought those craft classes would never be useful. Boy, had she been wrong.

She'd also learned a shortcut to making fondant. She just had to find some marshmallows, powdered sugar, shortening, food coloring and water.

"I'll be right back!" She ran out the door.

The best part of working at an exclusive resort was that they had a lot of specialty items. It shouldn't be hard to find the ingredients. And she was right.

Ten minutes later, she was back in the kitchen with the necessary ingredients. Krystof was busy scrolling on his phone. She set the box of items on the table.

"Make yourself useful and find me a mixer." She didn't wait for him to answer. She moved to the sink and washed up.

A few minutes later, she had a batch of fondant. She tried to remember what the topping looked like. It was flowers. Flowers were not easy to make. You had to make each petal, and that took tools that she didn't have.

"What's wrong?" Krystof asked. "Why aren't you doing anything?"

"I am doing something. I'm thinking."

"If you don't hurry, this kitchen is going to fill up with the catering staff."

She glared at him. "You don't think I know that, but I can't recreate the delicate flowers the bakery made for the original cake top."

"Then make something else. Something easier."

"But then Hermione will know."

Krystof smiled and shook his head. "Don't you think she'll know no matter how you decorate the cake? There'll be a layer missing."

Though she hated to admit it, he was right. "Fine. How do you think we should decorate it?"

He shrugged. "How should I know? If it were up to me, there wouldn't be any decorations."

Why had she thought he would be any help? If she couldn't make flowers, what else could she make that would be rather easy and still fit the wedding's beach theme? She stared at the blue cake. And then she realized she'd come up with the answer—beach items.

"I'll make a sand dollar, a starfish and seashells. They can't be that hard, right?"

"I don't know. I guess not," he said dubiously.

And so she set to work dividing the fondant and then coloring it different shades. She left part of it white. She removed a rolling pin from the box as well as the edible markers. Boy, she loved working in this place that had a little bit of everything.

She consulted an image on her phone as she created it. When she'd finished making the sand dollar, she asked, "What do you think?"

Krystof lowered his phone to look at her creation. "Not bad."

She frowned at him. "Not bad? I'd like to see you do better."

"Okay. It's really good. Better?"

"Much." She laid the sand dollar gently on the top of the cake and frowned.

"What's the matter?"

"It just doesn't look right."

They moved it around, and still she was certain they were missing something. She started to make a starfish. It was a lot harder than it looked in the photo. And considering she didn't have the right shaping tools, she had to make do with what she found in the kitchen.

"I've got it." Krystof started for the door.

She paused as she was about to cover the starfish with granulated sugar. "Where are you going?"

"I have an idea. I'll be right back." Without waiting for her to say another word, he dashed out the door.

She had no idea what he found so urgent at this moment. But she didn't have time to worry about him. She had her own issues. Like making the top of the cake look presentable. Her art skills were not the best—at least she didn't think so.

And though she wanted to cry in frustration, she kept working—kept trying to make the best collection of seashells possible from fondant. She'd make as many as she could and then pick the best ones to place on the cake.

She didn't know how long she continued to work while Krystof was off on his errand, but finally he returned. He stepped up next to her at the counter and perused her work. He was very quiet. Was that a bad sign?

With nerves frazzled, she asked, "Are they that bad?"

"Bad? No. I think they're great."

She glanced at him, at the edible seashells and then back at him. He wasn't smiling or laughing. In fact, he looked quite sincere. "Are you being honest?"

His gaze met hers. "Of course I am. You don't agree?"

"I think there's nothing I could create that would replace the beautiful flowers that were on the original cake top, but these will have to do."

"I disagree. This is going to be much better."

"I don't know about that." She stared at the

decorations she'd created. "I feel like there's something missing." She was so worried that she was about to mess up her best friend's wedding, and then she'd never forgive herself.

Krystof reached for a bag of brown sugar and the granulated sugar. He mixed them together. And then he carefully sprinkled it on top of the cake.

"What are you doing?" She moved closer to him. "Wait. Is that supposed to be sand?"

He smiled as he turned to her. "You did say it was a beach theme. And what is a beach without sand?"

"You're brilliant." She reached out and hugged him. "It pulls it all together."

The movement had been an automatic response. She turned her head ever so slightly and breathed in the slight scent of soap mixed with his masculine scent. *Mmm...*

CHAPTER SEVENTEEN

THE SENSUOUS TIMBRE of the violins filled the air.

This was it. It was time for the ceremony.

Adara turned to her friend. "Are you ready for this?"

Hermione's face lit up with a brilliant smile. "I definitely am."

"You look beautiful. I hope Atlas knows how lucky he is."

"Almost as lucky as me. Thank you for all you've done."

"You're welcome." She carefully hugged her friend, trying not to mess up her wedding dress or the styled curls that fell down her back.

Hermione pulled back. "Now you and Indigo better get down that aisle, or else I'm going to beat you to the end."

"You wouldn't."

"Don't tempt me. I can't wait to say 'I do.'"

They both laughed. It felt good to lose herself in the moment and not to think about her problems anymore.

"And I think there's a man waiting at the end of the aisle for you, too." Hermione arched a brow. "I've seen the way you two look at each other. It's a lot more than the fling you had going on before. I think Krystof really cares about you."

Heat swirled in Adara's chest and rushed to her face. "This day isn't about me or Krystof. It's all about you and Atlas." At that moment, the music changed. "I think that's our cue to walk down the aisle."

"This is so exciting," Indigo said. "Let's get these two married."

Indigo was the first down the steps to the beach in the artic-blue gown that showed her slim, tanned shoulders and gave a hint of her lower legs and the sandals they'd picked out. Adara waited until her friend turned the corner, and then she started after her.

When she turned the corner, she saw the sea of white chairs and the handsomely dressed guests. Her gaze moved up the center aisle to the flowered arch and then to the right, where the groom stood. Her gaze quickly moved past him to the best man, who was staring back at her. Her heart skipped a beat.

For a second, she let herself imagine what

it'd be like if this was their wedding. Would Krystof stare at her like he was doing now? Or would his gaze be warmed with love?

And yet the way he was looking at her now, it made her feel like the most beautiful woman in the world. For a second, she wondered if he'd look at her the same way if he knew she was broken on the inside. And then she pushed aside the bothersome thought. Today was for celebrating her friends' love. Tomorrow she'd deal with her diagnosis.

At the end of the aisle, she felt a gravitational pull in Krystof's direction, but she resisted the urge and instead took her position to the left of the aisle. She turned to watch Hermione approached them. She looked breathtaking. The pure joy on her face was the way every bride should look on their wedding day. In that moment, as Hermione stepped up to Atlas—as they stared lovingly into each other's eyes— Adara realized all the challenges of the past couple of weeks had been totally worth it. Hermione and Atlas got their happily-ever-after.

Hermione turned to her and handed her bouquet over so that she could hold both of Atlas's hands. As Adara took the flowers, her gaze strayed past Hermione and immediately connected with Krystof's. Was he still staring at her?

As they exchanged vows, Adara was utterly distracted by Krystof's presence. Any time her gaze would stray to him, he'd be looking back at her. What was up with him? Why was he being so attentive?

She looked so much like a bride.

He should turn away, but his body refused to cooperate.

Krystof couldn't keep his gaze from Adara. And then her head turned ever so slightly, and their gazes met. His heart started to pound.

She wore the most brilliant smile that filled his chest with warmth. It was as if she were the sun and he a mere planet in her orbit. He could imagine her walking up to him—being there with him.

Whoa! Where had that thought come from?

He reined in his thoughts. Sure, they were having a good time together. But they had a casual thing going. Why ruin it with a bunch of promises that would one day be broken?

After all, when the wedding was over, he would be on to his next adventure. This time it wasn't a card game. This time he was heading back to Paris. He'd made a decision. After his research and speaking with consultants, he'd determined the tech firm would be a worthwhile investment.

He would return to the island regularly to see

Adara. And he had hopes of convincing her to go on some adventures with him. They made a good pair. He hoped it would continue after the wedding. But for how long?

As the priest spoke of love and eternity, Krystof knew as sure as he was standing on that white sand with the sea softly lapping at the beach that one day Adara would be standing there in a white dress with flowers in her hair and stars in her eyes. She would be staring into the eyes of the man she loved. She would be staring at him.

Whoa! Where did that come from?

It was this wedding. It had him all out of sorts. When it was over, they could get back to the way things used to be.

And then the ceremony ended. Mr. and Mrs. Othonos started up the aisle. Now it was his turn to walk Adara up the aisle. He stepped forward and presented his arm to her. When she smiled at him, it stirred this unfamiliar sensation in his chest. He assured himself that it was nothing.

With her hand tucked in the crook of his arm, they were headed toward the patio area that had been reserved for the reception. Adara expelled a dreamy sigh. "Wasn't that the most wonderful wedding?"

"All thanks to you." And he meant it. "You

worked really hard so that everything was perfect for them."

"Thank you. But this wedding was a team effort. There were a lot of people that helped with the arrangements, especially you."

He shook his head. "I didn't do much at all."

"You did more than you think. You helped me sort out the dresses and pick out the music. And let's not forget how you helped decorate the cake."

"Huh. I did do a lot, didn't I?" He sent her a teasing smile. "What did you do again?"

She rolled her eyes. "Give a guy a compliment and it goes straight to his head."

He loved this side of Adara. That trip to the waterfall had done them both a lot of good. It had been an amazing afternoon—one he wouldn't mind repeating in the very near future.

She elbowed him lightly. "What are you smiling about?"

Should he tell her? He didn't see what it would hurt. "I was thinking about our day at the waterfall."

"You mean the day you had me playing hooky from work?"

"Oh, come on. You know you enjoyed it." There was no way he was going to believe that she hadn't. It was a day he would never forget. "We should do it again."

He expected her to agree, but instead, she said, "Come on. We need to form a receiving line." She grabbed his hand to lead him to the spot where he needed to stand. "They're waiting for us."

As her fingers laced with his, a jolt zipped up his arm and sent his heart racing. It didn't matter how much time he spent with her—she still had this special effect on him. He was so relieved they'd patched things up between them. And he would show her how much he appreciated her presence in his life later that evening.

Just a little longer...

She could keep it together a little longer.

Adara was indeed happy for her friends, but the doctor's diagnosis continued to linger on the edges of her thoughts. It was so much to take in. In an instant, everything about her life had changed.

She glanced around and spotted Krystof talking to a guest. At that moment, he glanced in her direction. When their gazes met, he smiled. It was a balm on her tattered heart.

She knew there was a lot more to her than whether or not she could give birth. But in this particular moment, it's where her mind wanted to dwell.

And yet when Krystof looked at her like he was doing now, she felt complete and whole. He made her feel like anything was possible even when she knew that wasn't the case.

Krystof was now headed in her direction. He stopped in front of her and held his hand out to her. "May I have this dance?"

"I… I don't think so." She had to start putting some distance between them.

"Come on. Please. I'm going to look awfully silly dancing out there all by myself."

"You wouldn't."

He smiled at her, making her stomach dip. "I'd do anything to make you smile."

And then he held one hand over his chest and held his other hand at his side as though he were dancing with an invisible person. He started swaying to the music. She couldn't believe her eyes. He was really going to dance without her.

People were stopping to watch their exchange. If she didn't dance with him, they were just going to draw even more attention. And she had promised herself that she was going to have a good time tonight—even if that good time was found in Krystof's arms.

And so she stepped up to him. He reached

out to her, and she walked into his arms. It felt so natural to be with him. It was though at last she was exactly where she belonged.

She corrected her thoughts. She didn't belong with Krystof. And he didn't belong with her. All they were having was a good time together. Nothing more. In the morning, he would leave on his next adventure. And she would be left to pick up the pieces of her life.

CHAPTER EIGHTEEN

THE BRIDE AND groom had departed.

The reception was over.

Krystof had just finished talking to Prince Istvan when he noticed Adara across the room. She was at the buffet speaking with one of the staff, who was clearing the serving dishes. Once she finished her talk, instead of heading toward the lingering guests, she turned toward the kitchen.

He followed her. When he stepped in the kitchen, it was abuzz with staff rushing to clean up so they could head home. There was no sign of Adara. Had she slipped out the back way? Was she trying to avoid him?

He knew she'd been a bit quiet and more reserved than normal during the reception, but he wrote that off to exhaustion. She'd worked so hard to make the wedding the best it could be that she'd worn herself out.

He turned and exited the kitchen. He made

his way to Adara's room. He told himself that he needed to make sure she was feeling all right, and then he'd let her get some rest.

He raised his hand and knocked on the door. No response. After a moment, he knocked again. "Adara, it's me. I just came to check on you." He knocked one last time. "Adara, please open the door."

He heard the click of the lock, and then the door swung open. Adara stood there with her hair down and her makeup smudged. Wait. Had she been crying?

"What do you want?" she asked.

He stepped past her into the darkened room, where only the large-screen television cast light. He turned back to her. "What's wrong?"

"Nothing's wrong. The wedding was a success. Hermione and Atlas are happy newlyweds."

She was saying all the right things, but he didn't believe her. He stepped up to her and gazed into her bloodshot eyes. "Adara, what's wrong?"

"Why do you keep asking me that? I answered already."

His gaze searched hers. "But did you? Really? Because I think something has been bothering you all evening. No. Make that since yesterday at dinner. You've been doing your best to cover it up, but there's something wrong. If it's about me leaving tomorrow, I've been giving that some thought."

Her brows gathered. "What are you talking about?"

"I'm talking about me starting to put down roots. I have to fly to Paris briefly but I'll return. Then I could stay here for a while and work on expanding MyPost. It was so helpful with finding the dresses that I think with the right leadership, the site could do a lot of good for so many more people."

"And you're going to—what? Live here at the resort?"

He smiled and nodded. "For a while. And while I'm here, I'm hoping we could spend more time together. We can see where things go with us."

"No." The two-letter word had a big crescendo.

Krystof's eyes widened. "Isn't that what you've wanted all of this time? I thought you wanted a committed relationship. I thought you wanted me staying in one place for more than a week at a time."

"No." She waved him off as though she were frustrated. "I mean, yes, but not now."

If he'd thought there might be a problem before, he was certain of it now. "Adara, talk to me. What's going on?"

Her fine brows drew together as her lips pursed together. For a moment, she stood there silently glaring at him. "Why are you pushing this?"

"Because I care."

Her eyes momentarily widened. "You do?"

He nodded. "You can talk to me."

He'd never let his guard down long enough to admit that he cared about anyone before, but he got the feeling Adara really needed to hear it tonight.

She sighed. Her shoulders drooped as though they were bearing the weight of the world upon them. He couldn't imagine what had her so worked up.

"Why don't we go out on the balcony?" He gestured for her to lead the way.

For once, she didn't put up an argument, but instead she moved to the balcony high above the now-closed pool area. It was a tranquil spot. He filled a glass with water and followed her. She took a seat in one of the cushioned chairs.

He handed her the water. "Thank you." She took a sip before setting it aside. "Maybe I should head back to the kitchen and make sure there are no problems."

"They have everything under control."

"How do you know?"

"Because I went in there looking for you. And they looked like they knew exactly what they were doing. All you need to do is sit here and tell me what's going on with you."

Adara opened her mouth as though to argue the point but then wordlessly pressed her lips together. "I don't know why you brought me out here. There's really nothing to talk about."

"And I think that is the biggest understatement I've ever heard." He wanted to push her for answers, because he was concerned, but he resisted the urge. The more he pushed, the more she'd shut down on him. And so he sat there quietly staring down at the pool.

After several minutes of silence, she sighed. "You aren't going to move until we talk, are you?"

"I'm not leaving until I'm sure you're okay. If that means we talk a bit, I'm good with that. If you want to sit here quietly and drink your water, I'm fine with that, too."

Her gaze narrowed. "Since when are you so Zen?"

A smile pulled at the corners of his lips. "Zen, huh?"

"Don't let it go to your head." She took another sip. "I can't believe you're holding me hostage."

He arched a brow. "A little melodramatic, don't you think?"

She set aside the water. "You just don't understand."

"I would if you talked to me. Don't you think after all we've shared that you can trust me?"

She hesitated as though she had to actually give the answer to that question some serious thought. His pride was pricked. Because no matter what he had or hadn't done, he had never betrayed her. And he never would.

"Adara?" His voice was filled with disbelief.

"Okay. Yes, I trust you."

"Then talk to me. If I can help, you have to know that I'll do it."

She shook her head. "That's just it. No one can help."

Had there been a wave of emotion in her voice? He turned to look into her eyes, and that's when he saw the gloomy look on her face. Whatever was weighing on her mind was serious.

"I care about you," he said. "And I'll support you through whatever this is."

She got to her feet and moved to the railing. "I can't have children."

Had he heard her correctly? Maybe she'd said she *wanted* to have children. The thought had the breath catching in his lungs. Children were not something he'd ever considered in his life.

Still, this wasn't about him. This was about Adara and her desires. And he needed to keep his promise to be there for her, no matter the subject.

He stood and moved next to her. In a soft voice, he said, "What has you thinking about this?"

Her face grew pale. "Does it matter?"

"Yes. It matters to you, so it matters to me."

"Please stop. Stop being so understanding. So caring." Her voice wavered with emotion.

He reached out to where she had her hand resting on the railing. He placed his hand over hers. "I think life happens, and we have to deal with it as it comes to us."

She struggled to keep her composure.

He was being so nice to her. She didn't know what to think.

Adara didn't dare turn her head to look at Krystof. She knew if she looked into his eyes, she'd lose the little control she had on her emotions. She didn't know he could be so understanding.

"I don't even know where to start," she said.

"At the beginning usually helps."

It felt strange discussing something so distinctively female with a man. And yet she knew that whatever she discussed with Krystof wouldn't go any further. He'd proved that over and over again.

"It started when I missed my monthly."

Krystof remained quiet. Very quiet. But he didn't remove his hand from hers.

"I knew I wasn't pregnant, because you were the only person I'd been with in a really long time. And I'd had it since the last time we were together. But as one month passed without it and then two, I knew something was terribly wrong."

"And I didn't make things easy for you. I'm sorry."

She shook her head. "It wasn't your fault. You had no idea that I had a medical issue."

"Maybe if I had slowed down, I would have realized you were dealing with something."

She glanced at him and saw the serious look on his face. "Don't blame yourself. Even if you had noticed back then, I wouldn't have talked to you about it. Back then I was still in denial about what was happening."

"Which is what?"

"Well, the doctor said it could have been a lot of things. And so they ran a bunch of tests. It took a while for them to all come back. Yesterday, I met with my doctor."

"That's where you went?"

She nodded. "They wouldn't give me the results over the phone. I had to go to the office.
I know I probably shouldn't have done it the
day before the wedding, but I just couldn't wait
any longer."

"Of course you should have gone. I just wish
you'd have said something to me. I would have
gone with you."

She shook her head. "It was something I needed
to do on my own." She drew in a deep brew. "I
found out that I have early-onset menopause."

He paused for a moment as though digesting
this information. "And this is the reason you
can't have children?"

She nodded once more. "I think my mother
had it, and now I have it. I... I didn't even know
if I wanted to have children." Her voice wavered with emotion. "I mean, I thought maybe
someday if I met the right person, I might have
a family with them. But now that decision is
out of my control." Her vision blurred with unshed tears.

"Can they reverse this menopause?"

She shook her head as the tears spilled onto
her cheeks.

Krystof reached out and pulled her into his
arms. She didn't want to need his hug, but she

longed for the reassurance that everything was going to be all right.

And so she let herself be drawn into his embrace. Her arms wrapped around his trim waist as her cheek landed on his shoulder. Her face nuzzled into the curve of his neck. She inhaled his masculine scent mingled with a whiff of spicy cologne.

In that moment, she was distracted from her sorrow, and instead she lived in the moment. Her heart pitter-pattered quickly. And just as quickly, she remembered that she would never make anyone the perfect partner, because she was only a part of whom she'd once been.

She pulled away. "I'm sorry. I shouldn't have cried on your shoulder."

"My shoulder is there for you any time you need it."

She had to keep her emotions under control. She couldn't let herself fall apart and have him put the pieces back together. He was at last understanding that he had options if he put down roots—he could have a family of his own. Just not with her.

He studied her for a moment. "And now it all makes sense."

"What makes sense?" She had no idea what he was talking about.

"The reason you've been going out of your

way to make sure everything was perfect for the wedding."

"And what reason is that?"

He reached up and ever so gently tucked a strand of hair behind her ear. "Your body feels out of control, and so you felt a need to control every aspect of the wedding. I just want you to know that you can relax now, because you've accomplished your goal. This was the best wedding."

She hated how easily he read her. Because if he could figure all that out, he would also know that she felt inadequate and uncertain of what her future would hold. Would she stay at the resort forever because she didn't have any other place she belonged—no other family of her own?

The more the troubling thoughts crowded into her mind, the more her emotions rose. And she couldn't fall apart now. Not when Krystof was prepared to hold her together—to be there like she'd thought she wanted.

But now she couldn't be the person he needed. If they were to stay together, he might one day want a family. She couldn't give it to him. He'd feel compelled to tell her that it didn't matter. But it did matter so much that she felt utterly gutted. And someday it might matter that much to him, too.

"Krystof, you need to go."

"I'm not going anywhere. I'm here for you." He looked at her like he really cared. And it was making this so incredibly hard.

"I don't need you." She stepped back. "We're not a couple. We never really were. This is my problem to deal with. Not yours."

"Adara, why are you doing this?"

She was doing what was best for both of them. "Are you going to leave?"

"No. I'm not going anywhere."

Of all the times for him not to want to leave at the first chance. She knew if she stayed here, he would wear her down and they'd spend the night together. And in the morning, they'd be right back in this same awful position, because they had no future.

She didn't know why he was trying so hard. It wasn't like they were in love or anything. He felt sorry for her—that was it. And she couldn't keep doing this.

"If you aren't going to leave, then I am." She turned and went back inside the room.

"Adara, where are you going?"

"It doesn't matter." She grabbed her purse and keys before heading for the door.

"Adara, wait. Don't go."

She kept walking.

This time Krystof didn't try to stop her. He must have realized there was nothing that could be done for her. She was broken beyond repair.

CHAPTER NINETEEN

HOME AT LAST.

Her apartment didn't feel warm and comforting like she'd thought it would. It felt cold and empty.

Adara hadn't slept much that night. She already missed Krystof, and he hadn't even left the island yet. But he would soon be jetting off to some card game in a far-off location.

She hoped he wouldn't give up on finding someone special in his life. She wanted him to be happy, and she didn't think his nomadic ways would make him happy the rest of his life.

Knock-knock.

No one knew she was home. It had to be Krystof. Was he there to say goodbye on his way out of town?

She scrambled out of bed. She glanced in the mirror. Her day-old makeup was smeared. She had raccoon eyes. She rubbed them. It only smeared her makeup more.

Knock-knock.

Whoever was on the other side of the door wasn't going away. Adara groaned. She didn't want to see anyone.

"Coming!" In her shorts and T-shirt, she headed for the door. She swung it open. "Hermione, what are you doing here?"

"Good morning to you, too."

And then Adara remembered her manners and opened the door wide. "Come in. Shouldn't you be on your honeymoon?"

Hermione moved into the living room and sat down on the couch. "We're leaving today to visit Atlas's father, and if he's doing well, we're going on our honeymoon. But first, I wanted to check on you."

"Why?" Adara sat down, too. "What did Krystof tell you?"

Hermione's brows drew together. Concern reflected in her eyes. "Nothing. I haven't seen him this morning. But now I want to know what's going on with you two."

She couldn't hold it all in any longer. She needed her best friend. And so it all came tumbling out about her diagnosis and how Krystof wanted to stay on at the resort.

"So what did you say?"

"I told him we're not a couple. I… I told him we never really were." Her voice cracked with emotion. "I told him… I told him I didn't need him."

Hermione reached out and gave her hand a quick squeeze. "But you do need him, don't you?"

Adara shrugged. And then she gave in to the truth and nodded. "But he's finally figuring out that he doesn't have to be a nomad. He can make a home, have a family, if he wants. But I can't give him that."

"Did you ask him what he wants?"

Adara shook her head. "He would just say what he thought I'd want him to say."

"Would you want him making decisions for you?"

"No. But this is different."

"Is it?" Hermione arched a brow. "Or are you afraid to let yourself admit that you love him?"

"What? No. Of course not. We weren't a couple. It wasn't ever serious."

"And yet you two made sure that no matter how many miles separated you, that you saw each other regularly for months. I've seen the way you both look at each other. If that's not love, I don't know what it is."

It was true. She loved Krystof. She couldn't keep hiding from the truth. "But we're so different. I like to have my life planned out, and he doesn't even know what country he'll be in tomorrow."

"Have you ever considered another life—someplace far from Ludus Island?"

"No."

"Maybe you should give it some thought. I'll miss you, but we can video chat and visit often. The resort will always be home to you."

Could she be happy somewhere else? Could she be happy always moving around? She didn't know the answers.

Krystof had taught her that she needed to take chances and reach for the things she wanted. She had been thinking about starting her own event-planning business. Was now the time for her to be her own boss? Was it time to take a leap with Krystof?

It was time to move on.

And yet his bags weren't packed. He didn't want to leave.

Krystof rode the elevator to the penthouse. He wanted to say goodbye to Atlas before they both left. He had no idea when he'd see his friend again. He had a feeling it would be a long time before he set foot on Ludus Island again.

The elevator stopped, and the door opened. Krystof stepped off and found Atlas standing in the doorway to the penthouse. He waved him inside. "Come on in. Hermione isn't here right now."

Krystof stepped forward, coming to a stop right inside the doorway. "I won't take much of your time. I just wanted to wish you the best. And let you know that I'm getting ready to leave."

"Thanks for all you did. We both really appreciate everything you and Adara did for us and the wedding. So where are you off to? The Riviera? The Orient?"

He shrugged. "I don't know."

"You don't know? I know you like to be spontaneous, but don't you need a destination before you get on your jet?"

"I'll figure something out." There was no place he wanted to go. That had never happened to him before. He wasn't even excited about purchasing the tech company in Paris anymore. He just knew he couldn't stay here, not after learning that Adara didn't want a future with him. "I won't be back for a while."

"What happened with you and Adara? I thought you two were getting along really well."

Krystof blew out a breath as he leaned back against the doorjamb. "I thought so, too. And then when I told her that I was planning to stick around the Ludus so we could figure things out, she told me to leave."

"How did you tell her?"

"Tell her what? That I'm leaving?"

"No. How did you tell her that you love her? Did you include flowers and champagne?"

"What? No. I didn't do any of that."

Atlas waved him in the living room, where he went to the bar and poured them each some scotch. "Here." He held out the glass. "Take this. I think you're going to need it."

Krystof took the glass and took a healthy sip. "I don't know what to do."

"You need to tell Adara how you feel about her."

"Even though she already told me that we're over?"

"What do you have to lose? I don't know too many women who are willing to put up with your idiosyncrasies, but Adara has stuck it out this long without you stating your feelings for her. Maybe she's tired of waiting around. Maybe she thinks you don't love her."

"But I do." It struck him how easy it was to make that confession.

"Good. Tell her that. Don't hold back anything. And one more thing—when you tell her, don't forget the flowers."

"But will any of that sway her?"

Atlas looked at him pointedly. "Do you really love her? Are you willing to change for her?"

Krystof had been giving this a lot of thought. In fact, it's all he'd thought about last night. "Yes. Yes, to it all."

"Then why are you standing there wasting time telling me? You need to go tell Adara all of this before it's too late."

Krystof put down his glass. "I will."

"And by the way, she's at her apartment on the mainland."

"Thanks."

Krystof headed out the door. He wasn't good at romance. He had no experience at it. But he could do flowers. He would buy her all the flowers in the world if she would just give him another chance.

She had changed him. She made him want to stay in one place—to have a place to call home. He wanted someplace that could be their home.

CHAPTER TWENTY

HER HEART RACED.

Her stomach was twisted up in knots. And her thoughts were scattered.

Adara continued to pick out an outfit to wear when she talked to Krystof—if he was still on Ludus Island. For all she knew, he'd listened to her and left last night. And then she recalled Hermione mentioning he was still on the island that morning.

But would he hear her out? Would he give her a chance to apologize? She had no idea, and she couldn't blame him if he didn't want anything to do with her.

She chose a summer dress instead of her usual business attire. Instead of putting her hair up, she left it down. Instead of putting on all her makeup for a polished look, she applied foundation, powder, mascara and lip gloss. It was a very casual appearance. And though all this was a diversion from her usual routine, she looked in the mirror and approved.

Change was scary and unnerving, but she could do it. She could move beyond the routine that she'd found comfort in for so many years. She could be something else, or do something else. It was in that moment she knew—with or without Krystof, she was leaving Ludus Island and going on an adventure. She had no idea where she'd end up, but the fun would be in the journey.

She wanted Krystof to join her. Not because she couldn't do it on her own, but rather she wanted to share it with him because somewhere along the way he'd become her best friend. He was the person she confided in, the person who inspired her to be more than she was now. And, most of all, she loved him.

She went to put on her high heels but then reconsidered. She dug a pair of beautiful sandals out of the back of her closet. She'd bought them on a whim and never found the right time to wear them because they didn't go with her business attire. But now was the right time. She slipped them on. They were so comfortable and looked adorable.

She searched the closet for a matching purse, because she liked things to be organized and matching. But she decided that not everything had to be perfect. Sometimes things just had to be good enough. She was good enough as she was.

Knock-knock.

Was Hermione back? Had she forgotten something? On her way to the door, Adara glanced around the living room for something that looked out of place, but she didn't notice anything.

She swung the door open and was greeted with a sea of red roses. Her mouth gaped. She'd never seen so many flowers in an arrangement. There had to be hundreds of them.

And she was certain there was a person behind them, but she couldn't see their face. Was it possible it was Krystof? Her pulse raced. He'd never bought her flowers before. But if not him, who else could it be?

The flowers lowered, and there was Krystof. "These are for you."

She'd have taken them from him, but she wasn't sure she could hold so many flowers. When Krystof did something, he definitely went all in. But what did this mean?

She opened the door wide and backed out of the way. "Come in."

He stepped into the living room. "Adara, we need to talk."

"I was just coming to see you."

His eyes widened. "You were?"

She nodded. "I need to apologize for last night. I shouldn't have said those things to you and then walked out."

He went to approach her, but the flowers stopped him.

"Why don't you put those on the table?" She gestured to the small table in her kitchen.

He did as she asked. They took up the entire table. And then he returned to her. "I'm sorry, too. I pushed last night when I should have let you take all of this at your pace. I should have told you that I'd be there for you, no matter how long it took for you to make sense of your diagnosis."

Her gaze met and held his. "You'd really wait for me?"

He stepped closer and took her hands in his. "My life hasn't been the same since you danced into my heart on Valentine's Day. I thought I could ignore what was happening between us. I thought it would just flame out, but none of that has happened. Adara, I love you and I want a future with you—no matter what the future looks like or where it is."

Tears of joy stung the backs of her eyes. "But I can't even give you the family you deserve."

He gently cupped her face. "That would never change my feelings for you. I love you."

"I love you, too." She lifted up on her tiptoes and pressed her lips to his. Her heart filled with love for him. The warmth spread throughout her body.

And before she was ready, he pulled back. His gaze once more met hers. "Stop worrying about everything. I don't even know if I want a family."

"But you might someday, and I don't want to take that opportunity away from you."

"If we did choose to have a family, I would love to adopt. I was an orphan, and I would like to bring a child into our hearts and share a happy, loving home with them."

Adara hadn't even considered that option. She was so caught off guard that he had given this some thought. The idea most definitely appealed to her. "I would like that, too. But there's one more thing…"

"What's that?"

"We have to have someplace to call home—someplace we can return to after an adventure. A place to keep all our treasures."

He pressed his hand to his heart. "This is where I keep the greatest treasure—your love."

Her heart swooned as their lips met. Her life

would never be boring again, and she didn't mind that at all. As long as Krystof was by her side, she would always be at home.

EPILOGUE

New Year's Eve, Paris, France

IT WAS ALMOST MIDNIGHT.

Adara sat at the ornate desk in the corner of their spacious living room awaiting Krystof's arrival. The mail was stacked neatly in the center of the desk with a cream-colored envelope from the royal palace of Rydiania on top. Her chest fluttered with anticipation. She knew someone who was royal.

She reached for the silver letter opener. Excitement coursed through her veins. It easily slipped beneath the sealed flap and gently sliced it open. She pulled out the invitation.

She couldn't believe she—well, they'd both, been invited to the palace to witness their friends, Indigo and Prince Istvan, be married. Adara expelled a dreamy sigh. She was so happy that Indigo had found her very own Prince Charming.

And she wasn't alone. Hermione was now

happily married. And even Adara had found her own true love. How had they all gotten so lucky?

Since Hermione and Atlas's wedding, there had been a lot of changes. Adara had quit her job at the Ludus Resort. The decision had weighed on her, but if she was going to take chances, most especially with her heart, she also had to take chances with her career. She had to reach for her dreams. Giving up all she'd known, from her comfy apartment to her long-time job, was the scariest thing she'd ever done.

But now she resided in Paris, one of the most beautiful cities in the world. And she'd launched her very own business. She was now an official event planner with her own staff. She planned special events, from conferences to weddings, and the world was her stage. She'd traveled all over the world to some of the most glamorous locations.

Best of all, they'd been able to find a way to make both herself and Krystof happy. She could still have a career that fulfilled her, and Krystof didn't have to curtail his wanderlust, as he traveled with her when his work schedule allowed. And in the end, they had a place to call home—this spacious five-bedroom Paris apartment that was situated along the world's most beautiful avenue, the Champs-élysées.

Adara had taken great pains to take both of their tastes into consideration when she'd decorated it. There was a touch of classic flair mixed with some modern touches. It had been a tough balancing act, but she'd learned that some of the best things in life were worth the extra effort.

And they'd even brought a bit of Ludus Island to their home. Over the fireplace hung a portrait of the twin falls that Krystof had commissioned Indigo to paint. It had turned out perfectly and was a constant reminder of the magical day they'd spent there.

Their life had settled into a comfortable routine of new adventures. Krystof had bought the tech company he'd been eyeing and merged it with his MyPost social media app. The company was taking off with him at the helm, and best of all Krystof enjoyed the new challenges it presented him.

Speaking of Krystof, the apartment door opened and he stepped inside.

"And how was your day?" He crossed the foyer into the living room.

"It was really good. And you're really late. Problems with your meeting?"

"Actually it was just the opposite. We're expanding, and negotiations ran long."

"That's awesome." She smiled at him. "You're really happy, aren't you?"

He slipped off his coat and laid it over the back of a white couch. "I definitely am, with you in my life."

Her heart skipped a beat. "I was beginning to think I'd have to usher in the new year alone."

"The plane got grounded for a bit in Rome due to bad weather. But I would never let you celebrate alone."

She held up the opened envelope with a royal seal on the back. "Look what we got."

"What's that?"

"An invitation to the royal wedding." She beamed. "Isn't it so exciting? We're going to the palace for a royal wedding."

"It's not as exciting as this." He walked over and placed a leisurely kiss on the nape of her neck. A throbbing sensation spread throughout her body. "I've missed you."

"You were only gone overnight."

"It was still too long."

She reached up and caressed his cheek. "Have I told you lately how much I love you?"

"No." He sent her a serious look as he straightened. "You haven't."

She got to her feet. "Are you sure I haven't?"

"Very sure. The last time you told me was on

the phone this afternoon. And that was so long ago." He pursed his lips in a pout.

"My apologies. I love you from the bottom of my heart. Am I forgiven?"

"I suppose. Don't let it happen again."

"I won't. Did you get something to eat?"

"They fed me well on the jet." He glanced down at her work clothes. "I thought you'd be ready for bed by now."

"And miss the fireworks? Not a chance."

Krystof checked the time on his Rolex. "It's almost midnight."

"Let's go out on the balcony."

"I'm right behind you."

As they made it to the railing, they could hear the jubilant voices from the street below.

"Ten—nine—eight—"

She gazed up at her husband. *Her husband.* It sounded so nice.

"Seven—six—five—"

She was the luckiest lady in the world.

"Four—three—two—"

Her heart pounded with love—love she hadn't known was possible.

"One!"

"I love you," he said.

"I love you, too."

And then their lips met as the fireworks popped and sparkled overhead. This was going to be the best year ever.

* * * * *

If you missed the previous stories in the
Greek Paradise Escape trilogy,
then check out

Greek Heir to Claim Her Heart
It Started with a Royal Kiss

And if you enjoyed this story, check out these
other great reads from Jennifer Faye

Falling for Her Convenient Groom
Bound by a Ring and a Secret
Fairytale Christmas with the Millionaire

All available now!